W9-AYV-592

THE MEMOIRS
of
SCHLOCK HOMES

THE MEMOIRS
of
SCHLOCK HOMES

(A Bagel Street Dozen)
by
Robert L. Fish

The Bobbs-Merrill Company, Inc.
Indianapolis/New York

Copyright © 1974 by Robert L. Fish

All rights reserved, including the right of reproduction
in whole or in part in any form
Published by the Bobbs-Merrill Company, Inc.
Indianapolis New York

ISBN 0-672-51987-9
Library of Congress catalog card number 73-22663
Designed by Linda Holiday
Manufactured in the United States of America

Third Printing

All of the stories in this collection were previously published in *Ellery Queen's Mystery Magazine* and copyrighted as follows:

THE RETURN OF SCHLOCK HOMES Copyright © 1964 *Ellery Queen's Mystery Magazine*
THE ADVENTURE OF THE BIG PLUNGER Copyright © 1965 *Ellery Queen's Mystery Magazine*
THE ADVENTURE OF THE WIDOW'S WEEDS Copyright © 1966 *Ellery Queen's Mystery Magazine*
THE ADVENTURE OF THE PERFORATED ULSTER Copyright © 1967 *Ellery Queen's Mystery Magazine*
THE ADVENTURE OF THE MISSING THREE-QUARTERS Copyright © 1967 *Ellery Queen's Mystery Magazine*
THE ADVENTURE OF THE DISAPPEARANCE OF WHISTLER'S MOTHER Copyright © 1968 *Ellery Queen's Mystery Magazine*
THE ADVENTURE OF THE DOG IN THE KNIGHT Copyright © 1969 by Robert L. Fish
THE ADVENTURE OF THE BRIARY SCHOOL Copyright © 1972 by Robert L. Fish
THE ADVENTURE OF THE HANSOM RANSOM Copyright © 1973 by Robert L. Fish
THE ADVENTURE OF THE GREAT TRAIN ROBBERY Copyright © 1973 by Robert L. Fish
THE ADVENTURE OF BLACK, PETER Copyright © 1974 *Ellery Queen's Mystery Magazine*

THE MEMOIRS
of
SCHLOCK HOMES

Table of Contents

The Return of
Schlock Homes

It was with bitter thoughts that I trudged down the broad stone staircase of St. Barts that late afternoon of a cool September day in '62 and turned my steps in the direction of the modest quarters I had—so long ago, it seemed!—shared with my dear friend Mr. Schlock Homes. The day had gone quite badly: the cardiectomy I had performed that morning had seemed successful and yet the patient had inexplicably died. Far worse, the pretty young nurse I had asked to commiserate with me by sharing an afternoon libation had curtly refused my offer.

It was in a black mood indeed, therefore, that I tramped through the streets, recalling in my memory the last time I had seen Homes, and the vivid scene of that struggle on the rocky cliffs of the Corniche— Professor Marty armed with gleaming sword, and my friend with only a fragile bit of ashwood, and the hungry rocks below reaching up through the angry surf! And then, when the Professor had lost his balance and gone over the edge, that horrible moment when Homes, his last bow ruined, had gone to fling it to the waves and had also fallen to his death!

Schlock Homes no more!

Even after these many weeks it still seemed impossible. With a deep sigh that owed, perhaps, almost as much to the memory of my friend as to that of the young nurse, I turned at last into Bagel Street, came to our rooms at Number 221B, and clumped up the shadowy stairway.

The room was darkening with the growing evening, but sufficient light still remained for me to make my way to the bookshelf and remove my address-book without the necessity of turning up the lamp. I was in the process of tearing out the page with the young nurse's name on it, ripping it angrily into shreds and flinging the pieces from me, when a sudden sound gave me pause. Had I not been positive of Mrs. Essex's intense dislike of felines, I could have sworn that a cat was mewing in the room.

Turning, I searched the gloom of one corner, and there, to my utter consternation, sprawled a lanky figure idly drawing a bow across the strings of a violin and producing what was, even to my untutored ear, a reasonable facsimile of Zetzenbull's Suite Sioux. So grave was the shock that I am afraid my mouth fell open.

"Homes!" I cried, my knees weakening.

"Watney," replied my friend with a dry chuckle, "your mouth is open." He laid aside his instrument and drew himself lazily to his feet. "In addition, you are littering the floor."

"Homes!" I repeated, my eyes widened in shock. "You are alive! How is it possible?"

He eyed me thoughtfully. "When I was so careless as to fall over that parapet in Monaco," he replied after a pause, "I was fortunate in selecting a spot where some night fishermen were preparing to spread their nets for drying, pulling them taut before fastening them down. Professor Marty had already managed to free himself from the cords and was scuttling off down the beach when I arrived. Needless to say, a second tangling of their nets did little to soothe the fishermen, and by the time I could assuage their anger and climb back to the road, you had already disappeared. Upon arrival at the hotel I found you had taken my effects with you, and I was therefore forced to remain in Europe, although I was not particularly averse to so remaining."

"And what brings about your return now, Homes?" I asked curiously.

The great detective smiled at me. "What brings about your haste to tear pages from that small morocco notebook, if questions of motives are being asked? You enter the room and immediately repair to the book-case, take down your address-book, and violently rip out the pages. The only possible conclusion one can draw from your actions is that you are in dire need of the binding. Taking into consideration the season, one can only conclude that you have decided to go hunting and require elbow-patches for your hunting-jacket."

"Homes!" I repeated once again. "You have not changed!" I stared at him carefully. "But what brings you back to London? And are you here to stay?"

My friend walked over and raised the lamp, bringing into sharp focus his familiar and beloved profile.

"Why, as to that, Watney," he replied easily, "only time can tell. Actually, the need of an old friend was communicated to me and I felt it necessary, in his cause, to return."

"Homes!" I said, overwhelmed with emotion at his statement.

"Lord Epsworth," he continued, much as if I had not spoken. "Surely you remember him?"

"Of course," I replied. Lord Epsworth was an old

friend of ours whose eccentricity for having all neigh-
bors at a minimum distance of three miles from his
estate had brought this measure to be known in those
parts as the Epsworth League. "Just what is causing
his Lordship concern?"

Homes smiled gravely. "Later," he said quietly. His
keen eyes surveyed me. "You appear a bit under the
weather, Watney. If you are free to join me in this case
I should be much delighted. I suggest that the fresh
air of the highlands may be just the prescription you
require for the obvious disappointment of missing
your hunting."

"I should like that, Homes!" I cried.

"Good. Then I suggest you pack without delay, for
in anticipation of your acceptance I have booked us
space on the Glasgow Express which leaves Euston
within the hour."

I went to my room and began throwing clothes into
my old campaign bag, the young nurse now forgotten.
The thought of Homes's return, and his request for
my help on a case, was like wine to me. Feeling better
by the moment, I joined Homes in the living-room and
we descended together to take a hansom to the station.

We arrived in good time, and once seated in our
compartment Homes lit a Bulgarian and leaned back,
flicking ashes on the floor. I smiled at the well-
remembered gesture.

"This is like old times, Homes," I remarked warmly.
"It has been some time since a case has taken us above
the Scottish border."

"It has indeed," he conceded. "The last time was
when we were so fortunate as to prevent warfare

4

among some of the eminent Scottish families, when their tempers got the better of their judgement."

I nodded, recalling the case well. In my notes it still remains waiting to be delineated, bearing the title of *The Adventure of the Steamed Clans.*

"Well do I remember, Homes," I said, and then leaned forward. "But enough of these memories. If you don't mind, please favor me with the details of Lord Epsworth's problem."

A frown crossed my friend's face. He reached forward, crushing his cigarette out against the carriage window-sill, and turned to me in all seriousness.

"The facts are these, Watney. As you know, Lord Epsworth is the owner of a famous pig, known to all fanciers as the Duchess of Bloatings, and winner of countless medals and ribbons. Well, to be blunt, the Duchess of Bloatings is missing. Upon learning of his loss, Lord Epsworth immediately instituted a search, and even managed to engage the services of a wandering band of gypsies he had allowed to camp on his grounds, as the Duchess of Bloatings seemed particularly partial to the refuse their campsite offered.

"But all to no avail. When, as of last evening, no sign of the missing animal had been noted, he thought to advise the local constabulary, who in turn made contact with Scotland Yard, who got in touch with the Sûreté-Générale, who managed to locate me. It is for the purpose of finding the missing prize-winning pig that we are travelling north."

I nodded my head in understanding. "Tell me, Homes, do you have any theories on the matter?"

"None," he replied honestly. "Until we are upon the actual scene, I fear there is little to do. I suggest

5

we dine and then have the attendant make up our beds. My trip from the Continent was quite tiring, and we shall have need for clear heads to-morrow!"

The following morning we engaged a trap at the station and drove through the sparkling Scottish sunlight to Bloatings, the home of Lord Espworth and—until recently—his prize pig as well. We found his Lordship puttering in the garden, using an old woodshafted putterer of a type long out of style below the border. At sight of the two of us he dropped the club and hurried forward, peering at us queryingly through his thick spectacles.

"Homes!" he cried at last in recognition. "You have come!" He paused. "But why?"

"The Duchess of Bloatings," Homes replied imperturbably.

"A beautiful animal," his Lordship stated, nodding his head. But then his face fell and he added sadly, "But she is missing."

"I know," Homes said gently. "You asked me to investigate."

"I did? That's right, I did, didn't I? Come, let us repair to the study and I shall give you all the details of this foul kidnapping!" He paused uncertainly, staring about. "Now, where is the study?"

Homes, as usual, was able to supply the answer to the question, and moments later we found ourselves seated in the vast library and being served coffee.

"And now, Lord Epsworth," Homes said calmly, putting down his cup, "the details, if you please."

"Of course," his Lordship said, smiling agreeably. "The details . . . of what, Homes?"

"The loss of your pig," Homes reminded him.

"Oh! Yes! Well, it seems that about two evenings ago—or it may have been three—or was it four?—the trainer, Jerkins, went to feed the Duchess and she wasn't there. Most unusual, I assure you. She was often late for shows, and occasionally for fairs, but never for meals. Jerkins looked about, of course, but he failed to spot her. Eventually he told me, and I also looked for her, but to tell the truth I'm rather nearsighted. Actually," his Lordship said sadly, "we never did find her."

Homes nodded thoughtfully. "Is there any possibility she may have merely wandered away?"

"The Duchess?" His Lordship shook his head. "She weighed over twenty-two stone. Normally she had trouble standing, let alone wandering."

"I see. Tell me, your Lordship, do you recall anything out of the ordinary that may have occurred that evening? Or any unusual sound that might lend itself as some sort of clew?"

Lord Epsworth thought deeply for several moments. "Possibly the word 'unusual' is too strong," he said at last, "particularly since it happened every day. But I do seem to recall the cook's children singing one of their little nursery rhymes. I had quite a time understanding Jerkins at first, the little ones made so much noise!"

A sudden gleam appeared in my friend's eyes. "Nursery rhyme?" he asked softly. "Very interesting! From the mouths of babes, you know, Lord Epsworth.

7

. . . Can you recall exactly which nursery rhyme they were singing?"

Lord Epsworth frowned. "Let me see . . ." Suddenly he looked up, his eyes bright. "By Jove, Homes, you are amazing! Now that I remember, they were singing some song about pig-stealing!"

"Ah!" Homes said in satisfaction. "And where might I find these children?"

Lord Epsworth's face fell. "In London, I'm afraid. They are off on a holiday to their home in the section of Stepney." His faced cleared as one mystery, at least, was resolved for him. "So that's why it's been so quiet here lately!"

Homes disregarded this. "Then we shall have to solve the case without their help," said he, and springing to his feet he began to pace before the library shelves, peering intently at the titles facing him.

Suddenly he withdrew a book and began to study its contents. When he turned to us there was a smile of satisfaction upon his face.

"Can this be the nursery rhyme the children were singing, your Lordship?" he inquired, and began reading aloud:

" 'Tom, Tom, the piper's son
    Stole a pig and away he run.' "

Lord Epsworth sat up, astounded. "Homes, you are a genius! How you do it I'll never know! That was it exactly!"

"But in what way does it help us, Homes?" I asked, confused by the entire affair.

"That we have yet to determine," replied my friend evenly. He replaced the book on the shelf and turned to Lord Epsworth. "We had best get to work. I shall want a word with Jerkins and a look about. As soon as I have news for you, I shall be back."

"Do that," said his Lordship heartily, and then paused. "And when you are speaking with Jerkins, ask him if he's seen the Duchess of Bloatings about anywhere, will you?"

Without further conversation we left the library and made our way towards the sties that constituted Jerkins' domain. Until now I had held my tongue, but I thought I saw the solution to the mystery and could not refrain from voicing it.

"You know Lord Epsworth as well as I do, Homes," I said simply. "In my opinion he did not lose this pig, he merely misplaced her!"

Homes shook his head. "The thought had also occurred to me, Watney, but a twenty-two-stone pig is difficult to misplace. Besides, you are forgetting the nursery rhyme."

"I fail to see what a nursery rhyme could possibly have to do with it," I replied with some exasperation.

"You shall," he answered cryptically, and turned into the pen area.

Jerkins was there, mournfully cleaning the empty pen of his lost champion, but try as he would to help us, the poor fellow had no useful ideas on the subject, although he did recall the children singing that evening.

Homes dismissed the man and turned, studying the surrounding countryside carefully. In the distance the camp of the gypsies could be seen, and with a brief nod in my direction, Homes started off across the moors with the camp as his destination.

The camp was typical, consisting of ornately painted

charabancs drawn in a rude circle about a campfire from which the odor of a succulent barbecue could be discerned. At our approach a tall, swarthy fellow rose from the group beside the fire and made his way hastily towards us, meeting us beyond the circle of the charabancs.

"Yes?" he asked truculently. "What do you want here?"

"Please forgive our intrusion," Homes said placatingly. "We are investigating the disappearance of his Lordship's prize pig, and we thought it possible that you might have noticed some strangers in the vicinity the night of the event."

The dark-faced man opposite us shook his head. "I have been asked before and I have answered!" he said with some anger. "Do you doubt the word of Tomás, King of the Gypsies?"

Homes hastened to reassure him, and with the man glowering at us threateningly we withdrew and headed back in the direction of the main house, although the delicious odor of the meal cooking over the spit made me realize we had scarcely eaten that day.

"You were exceptionally polite to that crude fellow, Homes," I said.

Homes nodded. "You must remember that the gypsies were at their meal," he replied. "It would have been the worst possible form to interrupt them. Besides, I am beginning to get a solution to this puzzling affair, and my time would be better spent in pursuing it."

While he spoke we found we had returned to the pen area, and Homes fell silent, dropping into a brown study, staring about him with a blank expression which might have misled others, but which I

10

recognized as his normal expression when his great brain was busy with an abstruse problem.

I could hear him muttering to himself, and suddenly I realized that he was softly repeating the children's nursery rhyme to himself. With a puzzled shake of his head he was about to leave when his eye happened to chance upon a mark in the dust at his feet, and instantly he was a changed man. With a muffled cry he fell to his knees and stared in fascination at the smudge.

"Homes!" I cried. "What is it?"

Without deigning to answer he reached into his pocket and withdrew his magnifying-glass, bending closer to whatever had caught his eye. I could see his thin figure stiffen in barely concealed excitement as he read some significance in what appeared to me to be a mere smudge in the dust. Suddenly he looked up, his eyes gleaming in a manner I well knew.

"This mark!" he cried. "Do you see it?"

I bent closer, but again I could make nothing of the slight smudge before us.

"What is it, Homes?" I asked, mystified. "Certainly it is not a footprint!"

"But it is!" he exclaimed. "It is! Not, it is true, from a conventional boot—but a footprint none the less! As you know, I have made an extensive study of the wooden shapes and forms upon which various Indian tribes mould their moccasins, for each tribe uses a different form. And I tell you, without any doubt, that this mark was made by a moccasin formed on the last of the Mohicans!"

"Indians, Homes?" I cried. "American Indians? Here? In Scotland?"

But my friend was paying me no heed. Once again

11

I could hear him muttering the nursery rhyme, almost as an incantation, while his eyes stared fixedly at the smudge before him. At last he nodded briskly and rose to his feet.

"Of course!" he said softly to himself. "I am a fool! It was all there before me!" He turned to me, his fine dark eyes brooding. "I am afraid we must be the bearers of sad tidings to his Lordship. The Duchess of Bloatings is gone forever. By this time she is undoubtedly aboard a sailing ship bound for the American colonies, stolen by the savages of the Chesapeake region!"

"But, Homes!" I cried. "Certainly you did not come to this conclusion on the basis of that single smudge in the dust?"

"That was but the final proof," he replied. "Remember the nursery rhyme. And the fact that the cook's children come from Stepney!"

"Really, Homes!" I said with irritation. "You speak in riddles! What brings you to this bizarre conclusion?"

"Later you shall know all," he said grimly. "At the moment we must break the bad news to his Lordship. It will be hard for him to accept, but at least he will not suffer the pangs of uncertainty, not knowing what has happened to his pet pig. At least he will not spend his days in vain hope, waiting endlessly for one that will never return."

Turning, he led the way from the sties, and we went back to the garden. There we found Lord Epsworth, and Homes gave him the sad news. His Lordship took it as well as could be expected, even going so far as to thank Homes for his efforts. As he took leave of us he wrung Homes's hand.

12

"It was good to see you, Homes," he said as we climbed into our trap. "Thank you for coming." He stared up at us through his thick spectacles. "And if you see the Duchess of Bloatings along the road on your way to the station, would you mind pointing her back this way?"

Once in our compartment in the train I could contain myself no longer. "All right, Homes," I said shortly. "You have been mysterious long enough. Please explain yourself and your rather odd conclusions regarding this case."

"Of course," my friend replied, turning to me with a faint smile. "I should have thought by now you would have seen the answer for yourself, for it was surely simple enough."

He leaned back, lit a Trichinosis, and began his explanation in that pedantic manner I had long since learned to accept.

"The Indian footprint was but the final step in the proof, Watney. The nursery rhyme was the first and most important, and by itself should have given me all the information I required to solve the problem.

"Let us examine the words those children were singing. They went: *Tom, Tom, the piper's son,* and so on. Certainly there can be no doubt of the Indian connotation: What other groups use tom-toms? I saw this fact fairly early, but still the question remained: Which Indians? There are, as you know, many different tribes scattered along the coast of the American colonies.

"The answer, of course, was easily discernible once I remembered that the cook's children were from

Stepney, born within the sound of Bow Bells, and therefore Cockney. *Piper,* of course, is the Cockney pronunciation of 'paper,' and the *Sun* is a paper published in the village of Baltimore. The discovery of the Mohican moccasin-print merely confirmed what I had long suspected—that this tribe was far more nomadic than their history records."

I stared at my friend in awe. "Homes," I exclaimed with admiration, "the time you spent away from London and from your profession has not dulled your analytical ability in the slightest!" A sudden thought occurred to me. "But how were these savages able to spirit the beast all the way to the coast without its making an outcry of some sort?"

"Most probably through the use of one of their many herbs," Homes replied thoughtfully. "The fact that the miscreants were able to silence the Duchess— that by itself should have led me to suspect the native cunning of the American." A faint smile crossed his fine features. "Possibly this very fact should be put to use. If you will allow me to suggest a title for this adventure, Watney, should you ever put it to paper, I would suggest The Adventure of the Disgruntled Pig."

I shook my head. "No, Homes," I replied affectionately. "This case, which leads me to hope you will return permanently to Bagel Street and to your profession, can only be titled *The Return of Schlock Homes!*"

It was the following week, and Homes had fallen easily into his old routine, when I came into the breakfast room one morning just as our page was delivering a large package to my friend, who was seated at table smoking his first after-breakfast pipe.

Homes waved me to a seat while he broke the seal of the bundle and extracted a large pig-skin portmanteau. With raised eyebrows he read the accompanying message and then passed it across the table for my perusal.

Dear Mr. Homes (the message read): *Lord Epsworth has told me of your solution to the mysterious disappearance of the Duchess of Bloatings, and in congratulations may I offer this token of my appreciation.*

The letter was signed: *Tomás, King of the Gypsies.*

"This is rather odd, Homes," I said staring at the letter.

"I'm not so sure," Homes replied thoughtfully. "Had I not been on the scene, it is possible that suspicion might have fallen upon the poor gypsy." His warm eyes came up to mine. "Do you know, Watney, at times the pleasure of saving the innocent can be even greater than the satisfaction of punishing the guilty."

"Amen to that," I said, and reached for the kippers.

15

The Adventure
of the Big Plunger

To my friend Mr. Schlock Homes, inactivity was the deadliest foe with which he was ever forced to grapple. At those times, when interesting cases were not forthcoming, he would lie slumped in his chair before the fireplace in our quarters at 221B Bagel Street, his eyes dull and unseeing, lighting one Armenian from another and allowing them to burn out in his fingers. I had warned him many times that the scars would remain, but when Homes was in one of his moods it was most difficult to reason with him.

I was most strongly reminded of this characteristic of his quite recently when, in the course of groping blindly beneath my lowboy in search of a missing tuppence, I chanced upon an old folio of my notes which had been lost lo, these many years! I immediately squatted back upon my heels to peruse it, the years and my tuppence instantly forgotten. And there, in my own scrabbled hand, I read the delineation of the early cases in which Homes and I had been involved.

One such period of inactivity, it appeared, had occurred in the year '29, and had been all the worse for having followed upon the solution of a problem which had been exceptionally challenging. At the request of the Moroccan government, Homes had spent the summer in North Africa tracing down an illicit cinema theatre which had been inciting the natives to revolt through the presentation of inflammatory films.

16

With his usual brilliant display of genius, Homes had eventually managed to trace the plot to an ex-German adventurer known as "Sahara" Bernhardt; the illegal theatre—called "The Desert Fox"—he had personally located and destroyed. Naturally, after such excitement, the dullness of a damp London autumn lay particularly heavy upon him, especially since there seemed to be no immediate clientele for his exceptional analytical powers.

On this particular day, however—a gray, rainy afternoon in October, as I recall—I returned from my medical rounds to find Homes a changed man. Where I had left him dull-eyed and bored, I returned to find him pacing the floor in barely concealed excitement, his eyes alive and dancing once again. At sight of me he smiled his old smile and extended a telegraph form in my direction.

"A message from my brother Criscroft, Watney!" he exclaimed. "He has urgent need of my services. At last my ennui shall end!"

I nodded in delighted satisfaction. Criscroft Homes, whose position in the Foreign Office was a bit difficult to define, was not only Homes's sole relative, but also by far his favorite. Many a time we had visited him at his club, where he usually sat alone contemplating his naval responsibilities or some other weighty military problem. For him to request aid of Homes was a sure indication of an interesting problem.

I reached for the telegraph form, but before I could take it there came the sound of footsteps upon the stairs, and a moment later Criscroft himself had entered the room, crossed it to shake our hands fervently, and in almost the same motion flung himself into a chair by the fireplace, frowning at us both. A moment later he spoke.

"I hope you are free, Schlock," said he heavily, and leaned forward as if the comfort of his accommodation were somehow alien to the seriousness of his mission.

"Free? I have never been more free!" Homes dropped into a chair across from his brother and looked at him with gleaming eyes. "What is the problem?"

For several moments Criscroft did not answer. He cast his eyes towards the sideboard as if searching for words. I hastened to prepare libations even as I covertly studied the two men. I could not help but note, as I muddled the mixtures, the startling resemblance between the two brothers despite their great differences in height, weight, coloring, facial features, and general appearance. In silence I served them and then retired to one side to listen.

For a moment Criscroft fingered his drink in thoughtful quietude and then, quaffing deeply, set his glass reluctantly to one side.

"Are you acquainted with Lord Fynch-fframis?" he asked at last.

"The noted financier? Only by name," Homes replied.

"I am afraid you will never know him in any other manner," Criscroft said sadly. "He is dead, and a certain Silas Weatherbeaten, an American, is being held in custody at Bow Street on suspicion of his murder."

"Weatherbeaten? The American financial genius?"

"None other. And, I might mention, the colonial denies any part in the sinister affair. His Embassy has been around to us, and we are put in the position where we must either prove his complicity or release him at once. Needless to say, relations between our great country and theirs could become strained were we to make a mistake in this matter, and for this reason I wish to enlist your aid."

"Give me the details," Homes said simply.

"Of course. Well, the story is this: Lord Fynch-fframis either fell, jumped, or was pushed from his offices on top of the Exchange this morning at 9:45. At the time of the unfortunate occurrence, the only one present with him in his office was this same Silas Weatherbeaten. The American's story is that the two men had been talking when Fynch-fframis walked to the stock ticker in one corner, after which he gasped, turned pale, wiped his forehead and then with no further ado flung himself headlong through the window."

"The stock ticker? What is that?" asked Homes.

"I have no idea. I am merely repeating Weatherbeaten's words."

"No matter. It can scarcely concern us where the man walked just prior to the plunge. Pray continue."

"Well, Schlock, since there were no other witnesses, we have only Weatherbeaten's story to go on. Scotland Yard has been unable to uncover any history of previous enmity between the two men, but on the other hand they have also been unable to establish the slightest reason for Fynch-fframis to take his own life. As you can well imagine, the situation leaves us in the Foreign Office in a serious dilemma."

"I understand. And that's all you have to give me?"

"All except this." Criscroft paused to delve into a pocket, sorted through the conglomeration he extracted, and finally came up with a thin slip of paper. "When Lord Fynch-fframis was picked up, he was found to be clutching this strip of paper. To the best of our knowledge it represents a code, but a code so devilishly complicated that to this moment Department M5 has had no success at all in solving it."

At these words Homes's eyes glittered feverishly and he reached forward with eagerness, taking the slip from his brother's fingers and bending forward to peruse it intently. At the frown that appeared on his face I stepped behind him and read the puzzling message over his shoulder. It was neatly printed on a thin strip of yellowish paper and I reproduce the mysterious hieroglyphics for the reader's inspection.

$$\ldots \text{T-T } 7\tfrac{1}{2} \ldots \text{AllAf } 44$$
$$\ldots \text{AlRs } 12 \ldots \text{G\&F } 11$$
$$\ldots \text{T-T } 7 \ldots \text{AllAf } 43 \ldots$$
$$\text{AlRs } 11\tfrac{1}{2} \ldots \text{G\&F } 10\tfrac{5}{8}$$
$$\ldots \text{T-T } 6\tfrac{5}{8} \ldots \text{AllAf } 42$$
$$\ldots \text{AlRs } 11 \ldots \text{G\&F } 10$$
$$\ldots \text{T-T } 6\tfrac{1}{2} \ldots$$

"Well?" The harshness of Criscroft's voice betrayed his anxiety. "Can you make anything of it?"

Homes remained in a brown study, his eyes scanning the strange message. Then he raised his head slowly, a curious expression on his face. "At the moment, no," he said slowly. "It bears no resemblance to any other code or cipher I have ever seen."

Criscroft drew himself to his feet and stared down at his brother. "I am sure you have solved more difficult ones, Schlock," he said at last. "You are aware of the urgency of this matter. Should you require me, I shall be available at any time. A messenger can reach me at my club."

"Good." Homes came to his feet, extending his hand. "Be sure I shall get right to it!"

Once Criscroft had left the premises, Homes fell back into his chair, staring at the mysterious message with a fierce scowl upon his face, while I studied it over his shoulder. Suddenly a possible solution occurred to me.

"Homes!" I cried. "These odd figures could well represent street addresses! 'T-T' could stand for Tottenham Towers, and 'G&F' might well be the corner of Grantham and Frobisher Streets."

He shook his head slowly, his eyes never leaving the message. "I doubt it, Watney. I am familiar with Tottenham Towers, and as far as I know the apartment numbers run evenly. I cannot recall any Apartment 7½."

I attempted to bring to mind the numbering system at the famous Towers, but to no avail. Homes turned to his shelf of reference volumes and, selecting one, swiftly became lost in its pages. I waited patiently until, some moments later, he flung it from him with a barely concealed curse.

"Useless!" he muttered, almost in anger, and returned once again to his fruitless study of the flimsy slip of paper. At length he raised his eyes to me.

"I fear my recent spell of inactivity has dulled my brain, Watney," he said sadly.

"Never!" I protested as loyally as I could.

Despite his preoccupation, a faint twinkle had come into his fine eyes. "Or possibly it is simply that I am no longer used to labor," he said. "If labor is the answer, however, time can handle that." And drawing his chair to the table he began the series of permutations necessary to decoding the thin strip.

Dinnertime came, but Homes worked on. Our housekeeper, Mrs. Essex, was on holiday and I suggested that Homes join me at a nearby restaurant, but he refused. And when I left to eat, it was to leave him still at it, frozen in his chair, his eyes poring intently over the thin yellow slip, and his thin fingers racing across his scratchsheets . . .

I dined leisurely, knowing that when Homes was involved in a problem he did not particularly appreciate my presence. I had a brandy and cigar and then walked slowly back to our quarters. I mounted the staircase and entered the room to find Homes in conference with a ragged street urchin. The lad, of mixed Chinese-Israeli parentage, was known as Matzo-Tung and was the leader of the Bagel Street Regulars.

Together with Homes the boy was bent over a large street-map of the city, and as I entered both raised their eyes to me. I was shocked by the haggard expression on Homes's face; it was apparent that he had not paused for refreshment since I had left.

"Good evening," I said brightly, attempting to instill some cheer in the atmosphere. "Are you any forrader?"

Homes shook his head dispiritedly. "No, Watney," he said wearily. "I am reduced to clutching at straws. I have exhausted all other possibilities and am compelled to accept your suggestion that these strange hieroglyphics refer to street addresses indeed. The Bagel Street Regulars will check them out for me. Should this last lead be barren, I fear I shall be forced to confess failure!" With a sigh he turned to the young ragamuffin.

"Your instructions are clear?"

"Raht, Guv'nor."

"One lad to each address," Homes said sternly, "and the name of the tenant back here as quickly as possible."

"Raht, Guv'nor," said the lad and moved to the door.

"And mind the stairs," I said absently as he reached for the knob.

"The apples? I'll take 'em cheesy, Guv'nor."

He started to turn the knob, then paused with an odd expression on his face, and I saw that he was staring over my shoulder at Homes. I turned and to my amazement I saw that my friend was waving his hands frantically, his face distorted. I hurried to his side.

"Homes!" I cried anxiously. "Are you all right?"

"All right? I am a fool! What a fool I am! You, lad! Forget your errand! And here's a shilling for your trouble!"

Homes turned to me; all traces of weariness fled from his face, as the puzzled street urchin took the coin and slipped down the steps. "Watney! One moment while I change to proper clothing and we are off to visit my brother. How stupid I have been!"

And with no further comment he dashed from the room, removing his dressing-gown as he went.

I waited in mystified silence until, a few moments later, he emerged from his room straightening his weskit, and a second later I found myself being propelled down the stairway. Homes waved a passing hansom to the curb and hustled me inside.

"Homes!" I cried, tugging my arm free and straightening the fabric. "You have discovered the answer to this problem?"

"I have indeed!" My friend leaned back and patted his coat pocket where the mysterious strip of paper now lay. His eyes gleamed. "But I do not apologize for my delay, for it followed none of the normal, or even abnormal, rules of cryptography. And why?" His eyes twinkled. "Because it was never meant to be a code!"

Before I could ask an explanation of this strange statement, his eyes went to his time-piece and then to the man on the box. "Driver! A shilling bonus if you have us in Curzon Street in eight minutes!"

We came flying down Park Lane and turned precariously into Curzon Street with squealing wheel hubs, and seconds later the driver was hauling desperately upon the reins as we approached the club of which Criscroft Homes was a member. Homes was on the pavement before we had come to a halt, had paid the driver, and was pulling me impatiently up the broad stone steps of the club.

He brushed past the doorman, nodded distantly to the cloakroom attendant, and turned into the library, where, in one corner, Criscroft sat moodily. At the commotion our entrance provoked, he came to his feet and hurried forward as quietly as he could.

"Schlock," he said in a low whisper, obviously torn between the club rules for silence and his necessity for our information. He glanced about. "Not here. Come!"

He drew us hastily from the room, led us through a series of narrow corridors, until we found the kitchen. There he ensconced us on hard chairs, seated himself, and spoke in a normal tone of voice.

"Sorry," he said quietly, and then added in more anxious tones, "Do you bring me the news I have been awaiting? Are you able to help me resolve my desperate dilemma?"

"I am," Homes replied with quiet triumph. He leaned forward, narrowly avoiding a scalding teapot. "There is but one bit of information I require in order to complete my case. Am I correct in assuming that Lord Fynch-fframis originally came from common stock? That he was, as a matter of fact, born within the decibel range of the Bow Bells?"

We both stared at him in amazement.

"That is true," Criscroft said at last, staring hard at his brother. "Although how you ever managed to deduce it remains a mystery to me! It was knowledge that was kept secret even from Debrett's. I only obtained the true facts myself less than an hour ago." He leaned forward, a querying frown upon his face. "But how can this information possibly aid you?"

Homes smiled. "You shall soon see." His smile faded, to be replaced with a most serious expression. "The important thing is that you may now, with a clear conscience, free Mr. Silas Weatherbeaten. He was but an innocent spectator to this tragic affair."

Criscroft's eyes widened. "You can prove this?"

"I can." Without further ado, Homes reached into

25

his pocket and produced the mysterious strip of paper. Brushing aside some crumbs, he spread it out upon a nearby bread-board. His strong, thin fingers pointed to the words, while his tone assumed that degree of pedantic superiority which was so usual with him when he was explaining the successful solution to one of his cases.

"When first I saw this queer admixture of letters and numerals," said he, his eyes fixed upon us both intently, "I attempted to solve it through the standard methods of cryptology, as well as through the application of certain mathematical formulae which I have been fortunate enough to develop personally. All my efforts—I can now freely admit—were without success. Then, in desperation, I was about to send young Matzo-Tung out on what would have proven to be a futile quest, when he happened to use a phrase that immediately clarified the entire affair to me. A moment's thought and the picture was clear!"

"But, Homes," I protested, "I heard every word the young lad spoke, and I can see nothing in his words that could possibly aid in the solution of this problem."

"Watney, you hear with your ears rather than with your intelligence," Homes replied cryptically. "Do you not recall the young boy saying, 'The apples? I'll take 'em cheesy, Guv'nor'?" His mimicry was remarkable as he duplicated exactly the heavy Cockney accent of the street urchin.

I stared at him in amazement. "But how could that possibly help, Homes?"

"He was using Cockney rhyming slang, Watney!"

"Cockney rhyming slang?"

"Precisely!" He laughed at my blank expression. "I can see that you are not familiar with the Cockney, Watney. He chooses many ways in which to express himself, and the most famous, of course, is his rhyming slang. In order to state a word, he chooses a phrase of which the final word rhymes with the word he is attempting to express. For example, the Cockney will say 'storm and strife,' when he wishes to say 'wife.' And many of them, with time, have come to even leave off the last part of the phrase, so that 'storm' becomes 'wife.' "

I stared at him. His eyes twinkled.

"Yes, Watney! Take our little ragamuffin this evening, for instance. Apples, of course, is from the Cockney phrase of 'apples and pears,' which means 'stairs.' 'Cheesy' means 'easy.' He was simply assuring you that he would go down the steps with care."

His face sobered. "The moment he spoke I saw all. The mysterious message became crystal clear. Come, let me demonstrate."

His fingers slid along the lines of the strange message.

" 'T-T' can only be 'Tit-for-Tat'—or 'hat.' 'AllAf ' is 'All Afloat'—or 'coat.' 'AlRs' is the famous 'Almond Rocks' that the Cockney uses to refer to his socks. And 'G&F' can only be 'Greens-and-Fruits' with which he designates his boots."

"Hat?" I asked, completely mystified. "Coat? Socks? Boots?"

"Exactly!"

"But the numbers, Homes," I said in bewilderment. "What significance can they possibly have?"

"Sizes, of course," Homes replied quietly.

We stared at him, considering his startling deduction. At last Criscroft cleared his throat and spoke. "But, Schlock—the numbers are continually decreasing."

"Precisely! And that is the answer!" The great detective's eyes gleamed; his deep voice became even deeper. "*The poor man was wasting away!* In all probability from some incurable disease. He was not wiping his brow when Weatherbeaten saw him this morning; he was undoubtedly trying to check the progress of his dread condition. And when he saw that it had not abated, but had even increased in tempo, he knew there was truly no hope for him, and that death was to be preferred to waiting until he was, quite literally, a shadow of his former self."

Words failed both Criscroft and myself at this remarkable demonstration of Homes's extraordinary reasoning powers. Impulsively I thrust out my hand in heartfelt congratulations.

"Magnificent, Homes!" I exclaimed, overcome with admiration.

Criscroft arose with shining eyes and placed his arms about his younger brother's shoulders in a demonstration of affection quite rare for a Foreign Office personality.

"Schlock, you may well have saved England another *cause célèbre,*" said he solemnly, and brushed the hint of a tear from his cheek.

Homes shook his head modestly. "Do not thank me," he said quietly. "Thank the Bagel Street Regulars or even Lord Fynch-fframis himself. It was his unconscious reversion to his childhood language when faced with a crisis that solved this case, not me."

"Nonsense!" Criscroft replied roundly. He cast his eyes about. "This calls for a drink. Cook!"

The following morning I was in the process of simultaneously attempting to reach for my Brussels sprouts juice and open the morning journal when Homes entered our breakfast room. He nodded to me pleasantly and drew up a chair.

Knowing my friend's desire for the news as quickly as possible, I forewent my vegetable tonic and spread the newspaper to its fullest. Black ink in profusion sprang to my eye; it took a second or two until the full import of the startling headlines registered upon my brain.

Homes had been reaching indolently for his napkin; at the sight of the horrified expression upon my face he paused, considering me wonderingly.

"Something that might be of interest to us, Watney?" he queried.

"Homes!" I cried, unfolding the journal further, and then doubling it to present him with the scarelines. "Look! The stock market has crashed!"

For a moment he hesitated, and then, after careful consideration, he completed the maneuver of placing his napkin in his lap. His fine eyes were warm with sympathy as he replied.

"Well," said he softly, "there is one consolation. At least poor Lord Fynch-fframis was spared the added pain of seeing his life's savings swept away in the holocaust."

I stared at him, a wave of admiration for his understanding flooding me.

"True," I said, and turned the page.

29

The Adventure of the Widow's Weeds

Two cases of exceptional interest occupied the time and talents of my friend Mr. Schlock Homes during the middle months of the year '63. The first, which I find recorded in my case-book under the heading of *Inland Revenue vs. S.H.,* deals with a personage of such stature that revelation of his identity could only be embarrassing and would serve no good purpose. The second, however, which I find in my notes entitled *The Adventure of the Widow's Weeds,* cogently demonstrates, I believe, the devious paths of Homes's ingenuity when applied to his famed analytical method of reasoning.

It began one pleasant Friday morning in early June when I came into the breakfast room of our quarters at 221B Bagel Street to find Homes rubbing his hands with ghlee, an Indian ointment he found efficacious for the treatment of his recurrent attacks of itching. At the sight of me he wiped his hands carefully on the draperies and beckoned me to join him at the window, where he pointed interestedly to the street below.

"There, Watney," said he with a twinkle in his eye; "let us test your powers of observation. What do you make of that poor creature?"

I stared downwards, following the direction indicated by his finger. On the sidewalk, shuffling along in an uncertain manner and pausing every few moments to peer hesitatingly at the house numerals, was a small figure who, from her braided hair, I correctly deduced to be a woman. I looked up at Homes queryingly.

"I'm afraid I am not at my best before breakfast, Homes," I said, temporizing. His expression of expectation did not change in the least. With a shrug of defeat I returned my gaze to the figure below.

"I suppose," I said after more fruitless study, "that you have deduced she is searching out our number and is coming here to visit you. Although," I added in complete honesty, "if this be the case, I must confess to complete ignorance as to how you reached your conclusion."

Homes laughed delightedly and placed an arm about my shoulders.

"Really, Watney," he said with pretended regret, "I'm rather ashamed of my failure as a teacher. Take another look below. Here is a woman who shuffles along on feet far shorter than normal for her height, who wears trousers instead of the customary skirt, who carries her hands across her body and inserts them into the opposite sleeves of her jacket, whose complexion is almond-colored, and whose eyes are slanted. Certainly there is but one conclusion that can be drawn from these observations."

"I *am* sorry, Homes," I said contritely, "but I really do need breakfast before tackling this sort of thing. What conclusion should I be drawing that I am not?"

"Obviously, that it is *you* she is seeking, and not myself. The pain of those poor truncated feet is evident from her shuffling gait; her tendency to try to warm her hands, even on a day that promises such heat as this one, is a common symptom of anemia. The almond complexion—as I am sure you will recall once you have had your first kipper—is a sure indication of liver ailment; while the slanted eyes, obviously caused by prolonged squinting, comes from poor eyesight and undoubtedly results in painful headaches." He shook his head. "No, Watney, this woman is seeking medical aid, not the aid of a detective."

I stared at my friend, open-mouthed with admiration. "It all becomes so clear and simple once you have explained it, Homes," I said in amazement, and then paused, frowning. "But, then, how do you explain the trousers?"

"Ah, Watney," he exclaimed, "that is the final proof! Any woman who dresses in such a hurry as to inadvertently put on her husband's trousers, and then having discovered the fact, does not take the time to correct the error, can only be driven by a need for haste more common to those seeking medical aid than to those soliciting advice."

He looked down to the street again and then smiled at me triumphantly, for the woman was, indeed, turning in at our street door. A few moments later, our page had opened the door of our quarters and was ushering in an attractive Chinese woman of middle age who bent her head politely in my direction.

"Mr. Homes?" she inquired.

"I'm Mr. Homes," I said, stepping forward. "I mean, I am Dr. Homes—or rather, I am Dr. Watney. If you will just wait until I get my medical kit, I shall be happy to attend to you."

She paid no further attention to me, turning instead to my friend.

"Mr. Homes? I have a problem which is of such an

odd and unusual nature that I believe only a man of your extraordinary talents can solve it."

Her English, to my surprise, was quite adequate and even made more charming by the slight accent. Homes acknowledged the compliment with a slight nod, then with a languid wave of his hand he indicated that she make herself more comfortable. She seated herself gingerly on the edge of a chair while Homes dropped into one opposite and continued to study her through half-closed lids.

"Pray continue," said he. "If I can be of assistance, be assured I shall be. What is the nature of this odd and unusual problem?"

"Mr. Homes," she said earnestly, leaning forward a bit without removing her hands from her jacket sleeves, "I am a widow. Until recently my husband and myself ran a small tobacco-shop in Limehouse where we catered in the main to the upper-form students at the nearby academies, plus a few sailors who dropped in from the docks from time to time. We even furnished a small room on the premises where the students could smoke, since of course it is against the regulations for them to do so in their dormitories.

"And then, Mr. Homes, about a month ago my husband died. Needless to say, it was a terrible blow, but the philosophy of my race is that life must go on. I therefore arranged for the services of a fellow Chinese to help me in the shop. He has proven more than worth his wage and keep, even adding a new cigarette to our line which he makes himself at night in order to keep our costs at a minimum, and the sale of which has surpassed our greatest expectations. Nor is he lacking in commercial instinct; he advises our clientele that his new cigarette is 'Mary-Juana,' two feminine names undoubtedly selected to appeal not only to the British, but also to the many Spanish-speaking Lascars who frequent the docks. And to appeal further to the sailing trade, he has named them—"

She paused and frowned in an embarrassed manner. "But I digress—please forgive me." She leaned forward again. "Mr. Homes, with our increased custom one would think my problems at an end, but in truth they are just beginning. For the past two weeks— ever since I employed this man—there has been nothing but trouble."

Homes raised a quizzical eyebrow. "Trouble?"

"Yes." She nodded her head sadly. "The students, who have always been most tractable in the past, are now quite the opposite, singing or fighting at the slightest excuse, and even becoming destructive, scratching their initials on the walls of the smoking-room with whatever instrument is available. One even attempted the feat with a banana and became quite belligerent when he failed to obtain legible results."

I could not help but interrupt.

"It appears to me, Madame," I said a bit stiffly, "that you require the services of the official police, rather than those of a private investigator."

She raised her eyes to mine. "At one time," she said softly, "not fully recognizing the problem, I thought the same, and even mentioned it to my helper. But he was quite horrified at the suggestion and insisted that Mr. Homes would be more suitable to our problem." She turned her head to my friend once again. "You see, Mr. Homes, he has heard of you."

Homes disregarded the flattery, continuing to stare

at her over his tented fingers. "You state that at one time you did not recognize the problem fully. I assume, therefore, that you do now."

"I do, but it is difficult to put into proper words. To me there can be no doubt but that my late husband's spirit is causing this havoc, that he is expressing his disfavor because I did not carry on his enterprise alone." She withdrew a petite hand from her jacket sleeve and raised it to forestall disagreement. "I know you English do not believe in ancient superstitions, but it is an integral part of our honorable doctrines. I am convinced that it is my late husband's spirit which is inflaming the students in their present ways. Obviously, the police would be of no help in this matter."

She hesitated a moment and then forced herself to continue, her eyes boring into those of my friend.

"Mr. Homes, I know that what I am about to ask is not easily understood, but I am desperate. Will you attempt to placate the spirit of my dead husband and persuade it to leave us in peace?"

I stared at her in amazement, fully expecting Homes to terminate the interview quickly and send the poor woman on her way; but to my surprise he failed to do so. Instead, he sprang to his feet and began to pace the floor rapidly, his hands locked behind him and a fierce look of concentration on his hawk-like features. At last he paused, turned, and nodded his head.

"I shall give the matter my undivided attention, Madame," he said. "If you will leave the address of your shop with Dr. Watney here, I promise you an answer in the very near future."

She rose, smiling tremulously at her unexpected good fortune, and pressed an already prepared slip of paper into my hand. Before I had a chance to suggest that my medical services were now available, she had closed the door behind her and disappeared down the steps. I shook my head at my friend in disappointment.

"Really, Homes," I said chidingly, "I am ashamed of you! Why do you promise such nonsense as placating the spirit of a dead man? Your failure can only lead to further disillusionment for that poor suffering soul!"

Homes stared at me calmly. "You noted that, despite her obvious infirmities, she still insisted upon discussing her problem?"

"Of course I noticed it," I said a bit warmly.

"Then they must play a role of such importance that we are forced to respect her desires."

"But still, Homes," I said, "to promise to placate a dead man's spirit!"

"I promised her an answer to her problem, Watney, nothing more. Tell me, do you believe in superstition?"

"Of course not," I replied disdainfully.

"Nor do I. The fact that the trouble started with the advent of this excellent assistant, therefore, must only be coincidental, and the answer must therefore lie elsewhere." He withdrew his time-piece and glanced at it. "A trip to the tobacco-shop after lunch is indicated, I think. A pity, though—I had hoped to hear that program of religious music at Albert Hall this afternoon."

"Religious music, Homes?" I asked curiously.

"Yes. The Suite Sistine is being sung there to-day. By the Beadles, of course." He shrugged. "Ah, well, duty before pleasure . . ."

I was quite busy that afternoon myself, having scheduled a trepanning operation to relieve a hemorrhage—a bloody bore, I might mention—and it was therefore quite late when I returned to Bagel Street and let myself into our rooms.

To my surprise Homes had not yet returned, but thinking it quite possible that he had managed to finish in time for the concert, I turned up the lamp and prepared to await his return with a bit of research. No sooner had I taken down the proper volume and opened it to the section on malpractice, however, than I heard the sound of feet coming wearily up the staircase, and a moment later Homes had come into the room and dropped heavily into an easy chair.

One look at his drawn face and I moved to the sideboard and began to prepare a drink.

"No luck, Homes?" I said.

"Nothing of any importance," he replied in a discouraged tone of voice. "I did manage to have a fast walk-around of the two main academies in the area, Twitchly and St. Pothers, and I also, of course, visited the tobacco-shop. Oddly enough, none of the students was present, which was equally surprising to our client, and I was therefore unable to interview any of the little—" He leaned over, accepted the proffered drink, then leaned back once again. "However, I did see the damage they had wrought in the smoking-room, and I must say the British schoolboy has improved greatly in imagination since my days at Wreeking."

"Improved, Homes?" I asked, mystified.

He chuckled. "Have you ever attempted to write your initials using a banana as a stylograph, Watney?" he inquired.

I shook my head. "I'm afraid it is scarcely an improvement to brag about," I said tartly. "In my days at Barbour College it would not have been considered cricket to destroy the property of others."

"Destroy? I thought it rather an improvement. The original wallpaper—"

"Still," I insisted, "I'm afraid in my day we would not have considered it cricket. Or at least not *very* cricket."

"You may be right," Homes admitted lazily, eyeing his drink. "But times change, Watney. To-day—"

He paused abruptly, and then sat up so suddenly that for a moment I thought his libation would be spilled in my lap. "Watney!" he cried. "You have it! Of course! Of course!"

"I have what, Homes?" I asked in bewilderment.

"The answer! The answer to it all!" He sprang to his feet, setting his drink impatiently to one side. "The evening journal, Watney! Where is it?"

"On the table," I replied, completely puzzled. "But I do not understand, Homes. I have the answer to what?"

But Homes was paying small heed to my query. In two strides he had reached the table and turned on the gas-lamp high above it. His hands found the journal, and he began turning the pages rapidly. Having at last found the section he wanted, he spread it open and began to run his hand rapidly down one of the columns. And then his rigid finger froze against a printed line and he turned to me triumphantly.

"Of course! I was a fool—and a forgetful fool at that. Particularly in view of the date!"

38

"The date?" I asked, now completely confused. "What has the date got to do with it?"

"As much as the reason why there were no students in the tobacco-shop to-day!" he replied cryptically. "Come, Watney! Explanations can wait! At the moment the most important thing is to relieve the poor woman's mind without delay."

With no further word he sprang for the door and was down the stairway in moments, rushing out to the kerb to wave wildly at a passing hansom cab. By the time I had managed to recover my wits sufficiently to follow, he had a jehu drawn up to the kerb and was bounding into his vehicle. His hand reached backwards, dragging me along, pulling me into the swaying carriage. As I recovered my balance, he fell back against the leather seat, his eyes gleaming excitedly.

"I only pray that we are not too late, Watney!" he exclaimed. "She must close that smoking-room at once, and hereafter keep it closed."

"But why, Homes?" I cried.

"Because all the trouble up to now was only leading to the culmination to-night! And why? Because we have been concerning ourselves with the wrong coincidence!"

I grasped his arm angrily. "Enough of these enigmatic statements, Homes," I said. "Pray explain yourself at once."

He disengaged himself from my grip and smiled at me faintly.

"Since the source of my enlightenment was a statement you made yourself, Watney, I should think explanations are unnecessary," he said, and then laughed aloud at the fierce expression on my face. "All right, then, you shall know all." His face became serious once again.

"To begin with, as a result of investigating the wrong coincidence, we were attempting to correlate the arrival of the new assistant at the shop with the troubles encountered there, whereas we should have attempted to correlate the troubles with the date."

"The date?" I asked, still mystified.

"Precisely. When you mentioned the word 'cricket,' and then were so kind as to repeat it, I suddenly realized that in all probability there was a serious rivalry between the students of the two schools, and a check of the journal indicated that to-morrow St. Pothers and Twitchly play for the Limehouse championship. And if the championship game is to-morrow, Watney, what has preceded it?"

"Examination week!" I exclaimed.

"Exactly. Well do I remember my own undergraduate days and the tensions that build up prior to final examination day. Combine this with the rivalry of the two top teams in the league, then put students from each of the two schools together in a small room at this particular time, and serious altercation is bound to ensue."

"But if examination day has passed," I objected, "why is it essential that the room be closed to-night?"

"Because of the game to-morrow! With the students freed of scholastic worries and intent upon building up spirit for the contest, the danger is even greater than before. No, Watney, the room *must* be closed at once. I only hope that we arrive at the shop before the students finish their supper and converge upon it."

"True," I admitted, and then frowned. "But why, then, should she keep the room closed *after* to-night? Surely the danger will pass once this evening is over, and besides, the students will be leaving for their holidays immediately following the game."

"They will, but within a few brief months they will return, and the ending of each half-term would only see a repetition of these unpleasant incidents. No, I shall tell her that her husband's spirit will only be placated by the permanent closing of the smoking-room. I shall tell her that her husband's untoward interference was not owing to her having acquired a new assistant, but because in his new state he has become convinced that academy students are too young to indulge in tobacco. In this fashion I shall resolve her immediate problem, and at the same time satisfy her superstitions."

I stared at my friend with admiration. "An excellent solution, Homes!" I exclaimed, and then paused. "But will not the loss of custom cause her to suffer financially?"

He shook his head. "If what the lady said is true, their new cigarette should develop sufficient trade with the sailors to compensate her for the loss of the students."

"I am proud of you, Homes," I said sincerely. "Never have I seen a case resolved with results so beneficial to so many."

"Thanks to you, Watney, and your inspired use of the word 'cricket.' I only hope we arrive in time, and that I have not overlooked anything."

The following morning, having finished my breakfast, I drew the morning journal to me and lit up one

41

of the new cigarettes which our Chinese friend had been kind enough to present to us in gratitude for Homes's solution to the case. However, I found the taste far too acrid for my palate, and I was in the process of crushing it out when Homes entered the room. He noted my uneconomical gesture with raised eyebrows and seated himself across from me with a faint smile.

"The new cigarette is not to your liking, Watney?" he inquired.

"I'm afraid not," I replied, and proffered him the packet. "Possibly you might care for them."

He shook his head as he idly took the packet from my hand. "No, I'm too accustomed to my Mesopotamians," he replied, studying the outer wrapping. Then suddenly his eyes narrowed and he stared at me with a fierce frown.

"Watney! Is there any report in the journal of trouble in Limehouse last night?"

I hurriedly turned the pages of the journal and then stopped as my eye caught the heading of an article. "Why, yes, Homes," I said, marvelling as always at his uncanny ability to anticipate these things. "A riot at the docks, actually."

He slammed one hand down against the table-top. "I am a fool! She began to tell us the name of these new cigarettes and then stopped. I should have insisted upon knowing!"

I reached over and picked up the packet, staring at it. "But I do not understand, Homes," I said, puzzled.

He leaned over the table, his eyes burning with excitement.

"No? Do you not realize, Watney, that this name is

an insult to every nautical man operating under steam, since it indicates that he is only fit to handle sail?"

Comprehension dawned on me. "Of course! And it is also a word commonly used to denote a midshipman, the bane of every honest sailor's existence."

"Precisely. We must telegraph her at once."

With a nod of agreement I reached for my pad of telegram forms, and under Homes's dictation I hastily scribbled the vital message. It read:

"Madame: You must immediately cease to call your new cigarettes Reefers."

The Adventure
of the Perforated Ulster

A hiatus in cases of any serious consequence during
the early months of the year '66 allowed my friend Mr.
Schlock Homes an opportunity for some well-needed
rest, as well as a chance to indulge in a few of his many
hobbies. I recall in particular how diligently he prac-
ticed his prestidigitation in preparation for the annual
Magicians' Meet; but I saddened to relate that when
it finally was held, poor Homes was found wanding.

The same period, however, permitted me to bring
some order to my voluminous notes, and it is well that
I did so, for two cases which I had planned on ulti-
mately relating turned out to be nothing of the sort.
Homes had been writing a treatise on the mating-
dance of the *ondatra bibethecus,* and I had somehow
mistakenly incorporated his notes in my case-book as
The Adventure of the Muskrat Ritual. An even greater
embarrassment was narrowly avoided when I discovered a long series of correspondence covering an un-
paid bill of Homes's to a doctor at a local hospital,
which I had erroneously filed as *The Adventure of the
Patient Resident.*

Time, however, permitted the correction of these
errors, and it was with a feeling of growing ennui that
I came into the breakfast room of our quarters of 221B
Bagel Street one bright morning in April to find
Homes already ensconced at the table, his creamed
kipper already finished, and lighting his first after-
meal Bulgarian. He smiled brightly as I entered, and

I noticed a telegraph form fluttering from his thin fingers.

"Ah, Watney!" said he, his eyes sparkling. "It appears our inactivity is about to end. My brother Criscroft has telegraphed that he intends to drop by this morning, and as you are well aware, such visits in the past have invariably led to the most interesting of problems. I trust this occasion will prove no exception."

"But he offers no clew?" I inquired, sitting down and drawing my napkin under my chin.

"He says—but never mind. Here, unless I am greatly mistaken, is Criscroft himself."

He turned towards the door, and a moment later our page had ushered in Homes's illustrious brother. With a brusque refusal of a kipper, Criscroft flung himself into a chair and stared at us broodingly.

"Schlock," he said at last, his voice heavy with worry, "I know that in the past I have often brought you problems affecting the well-being of our country; but believe me when I say that never before has one of our basic institutions been faced with so dire a threat!"

Homes leaned forward, his voice deeply sympathetic. "As you well know," he said sincerely, "I am always at your service. Pray, how may I be of assistance?"

Criscroft shook his head in misery. "I greatly fear," he said in a tone heavy with dread, "that we have a case of pilfering at our club."

Homes's eyebrows lifted slightly. "But, certainly," he said with a frown, "a simple case of pilfering should not upset you to this degree. Any club might have an unfortunate member who temporarily finds his needs greater than his means.''

Criscroft's face had fallen—if possible—even lower during this discourse. "You do not understand," he said, his voice almost breaking. "It is far more serious than that. Our club has *not* been pilfered. The pilfering, I fear, was done for the *benefit* of our club!"

Homes's frown deepened. He tented his fingers and stared across the ridge-pole of his knuckles into his brother's tortured eyes.

"You mean—?"

"Exactly! Were it to be bruited about that our financial status was so precarious that such assistance was necessary to maintain us, the mere rumor might easily shatter the confidence of the public in this staunchest of all our national institutions!"

"And you think—?"

"Indubitably! Were people to begin doubting the solidity of our British clubs, there is no predicting to what dark ends these suspicions might lead!"

"And you suspect—?"

"Definitely! It is obvious that the perpetrator of this foul deed is not doing it out of idle whim, nor would he take so drastic a step out of mere personal spite."

"And you conclude—?"

"Precisely! He is therefore acting under the orders of some group dedicated to the destruction of our system. Undoubtedly a foreign group, since no Englishman, however treasonous, would be so subversive as to attack the institution of the British club!'' A look of peace replaced the agonized expression on his face. "You cannot know how good it is, Schlock, to benefit from your analysis. And I am convinced you are right!"

"Thank you," Homes replied modestly, and leaned forward again. "Pray favor us with the details."

"Of course," Criscroft agreed. "Well, as you may or may not know, I have recently assumed the chairmanship of our club's House Committee, and in this capacity I have the responsibility for the operation of the bar and kitchen. I have therefore taken, of late, to inspecting the culinary premises at odd hours, in order to see how the steward is handling his duties."

He paused a moment to collect his thoughts, and then continued: "Well, about a week ago, on one of my periodic tours of the kitchen, I chanced to note a new coffee percolator. I said nothing at the time, but I later made it my business to go back over the Committee minutes, and I found no recommendation for the purchase of this percolator, nor, in fact, any appropriation by the Finance Committee for its acquisition."

"And you considered this odd?"

"Extremely odd, particularly since few of our members are addicted to the bean, considering it quite rightly a colonial affectation. However, I continued to maintain my own counsel, awaiting further developments. And then, just the other evening, in checking the bar equipment for our annual Walpurgis Night Dinner—Lord Walpurgis is our oldest member and therefore annually feted—I was amazed to discover a new cocktail shaker."

"A cocktail shaker?" Homes's eyebrows shot up.

Criscroft smiled grimly. "You also note the foreign touch, eh? As we all know, a cocktail shaker tends to bruise whisky, and no true Englishman would think of employing one."

"Certainly not!" Homes exclaimed indignantly. His voice became probing. "And I assume that again there had been neither recommendation nor appropriation for its purchase?"

"Neither. I knew then, of course, that the matter was far more serious than a simple error in judgement, and I felt it vital to seek your aid."

"And well that you did so! What is the name of this steward?"

"Sean O'Callahan."

A thoughtful frown crossed the lean face of my friend. "Not an English name," he said slowly.

"Now that you mention it, it does sound foreign," Criscroft replied, and then looked troubled. "It is my hope that Sean is only an innocent dupe in the scheme. He is the fifteenth generation of O'Callahans to serve in that position at our club, and I should hate to think of him as a traitor."

"Still," Homes continued, his eyes glittering, "I assume you investigated him?"

"To the limited extent of our ability. I have had four men from the Foreign Office on his trail for the past twenty-four hours, have had his telephone tapped, and have even had secret microphones concealed in his attic bedroom at the club. Unfortunately, the A.I.C. men who installed them apparently did the job backwards, so I fear they have been less than effective. He can hear us, but we cannot hear him. However, since the building is an old one, and fairly well inhabited by mice, I doubt if he ascribes too much importance to the additional sounds of our conversation."

48

Homes came to his feet, striding up and down the room, his hands clasped tightly behind him. "So to date you have been unable to earth anything? I mean, able to unearth nothing?"

"Only this," said Criscroft, reaching into a pocket and producing a small, thin pamphlet. "In the manner of the Purloined Letter it was cleverly concealed by simply leaving it on the top of his dresser, which I must admit is quite suspicious in itself. However, I doubt if you will find it of much use. Our code experts claim it is beyond their ability to solve."

He handed the small brochure to Homes, who instantly dropped back into his chair to peruse it. I came to stand behind my friend while he examined the publication, and I reproduce its cover below for the benefit of such readers who are still with us.

Homes studied the cover for several moments and then slowly riffled the pages; the small booklet opened almost by itself to a page which illustrated a variety of cocktail shakers. He then turned several more pages, noting the detailed and colourful drawings and photographs of the items therein, and then shut the pamphlet with a dark frown upon his face.

"Schlock!" Criscroft cried, noting his brother's expression. "What is it?"

Homes turned a worried face in his direction.

"You can see the extreme care that has gone into the preparation of this booklet," Homes said heavily. "Certainly they would not have gone to this trouble just to embarrass your one club. I suggest the plot is far more sinister, and that in all probability they have infiltrated many more, if not, actually, all the clubs of London!"

Criscroft paled. "No!"

"I fear so. However, the game is early on, and there still may be time to scotch their nefarious plot." He shook his head and stared at the pamphlet once again. "There can be little doubt that this plan is costing them a pretty penny. It would undoubtedly, therefore, help to know the source of their finances."

"Raffle tickets?" I suggested helpfully.

He shook his head a trifle impatiently. "No, no, Watney! A plan this costly would not depend upon anything as uncertain as the proceeds of a raffle. Besides, what would they use as a prize? They are already using all standard items as part of their scheme."

Homes came to his feet. "No, the answer must lie, at least in part, with this steward Sean O'Callahan. If

you will permit me to change to more suitable raiment, I should like to study this situation at first
hand."

For a moment Criscroft looked a trifle upset. "You
are not a member, of course," he began, and then
shrugged. "If worse comes to worst, I shall just have
to tell them you are my brother."

The Anathema Club, of which Criscroft had the
honor to be a member, was an ancient and sturdy
edifice located on the edge of Interdit Park, and as I
entered the hallowed precincts I felt, as always, a
touch of pride in just being British, as well as a wave
of fury at the miscreants who dared to jeopardize all
that the club stood for with their foul scheme.

Criscroft led the way to the pantry and then excused
himself, leaving Homes and me to our own devices.
With the briefest of glances about the tiled kitchen,
Homes made his way to the small attic room which
served the steward as a bed-chamber. O'Callahan, it
appeared, was out shopping, but two A.I.C. men were
there, pretending to dust the furniture, and Homes
nodded to them distantly before beginning his search.

From my position near the doorway I watched as he
bent to peer beneath the bed, examined the closet and
its contents carefully, studied the dresser drawers in
great detail, and then walked over to pick up an open
envelope which lay on the top of a small desk in the
corner. One of the A.I.C. men interrupted his task,
moving closer.

51

"It's only the morning post," said he with a faint sneer. "We've already gone through it. There is nothing of importance there, Mr. Homes."

Homes acknowledged the statement with a cool nod, but still proceeded to raise the flap of the envelope and withdraw the note contained therein. A small rectangle of greenish-colored paper fluttered to the desk as he unfolded the brief note and perused it. His eyes widened as he scanned the lines, and then went instantly to the small bit that had fallen free. It was obvious that only the greatest of effort prevented him from exclaiming aloud.

"Homes!" I cried. "What is it?"

With a warning glance in the direction of the two A.I.C. men, he shook his head meaningfully at me, and then quite casually slipped both the note and the small bit of greenish paper into his pocket.

"I don't believe there is anything more for us here, Watney," he said, winking at me. "I suggest we return to Bagel Street and take up our investigation in more comfortable surroundings." And he winked at me again.

"Homes!" I exclaimed. "You have something in your eye! Permit me—"

"Later," he said savagely, and strode through the doorway.

It was only as our hansom was rattling across the cobblestones of Upper Regent Street that he allowed himself to relax. " 'There is nothing of importance there, Mr. Homes'!" he said with biting mimicry. "The fools! An obvious clew under their noses, and all they can think to say is: 'There is nothing of importance there, Mr. Homes'!"

"But, Homes," I said, staring at him anxiously, "what was there of importance?"

"Only this!" he replied, and thrust the note in my direction. I took it and perused it rapidly; its message was quite succinct. *Sir* (it read): *When last you visited my establishment, you forgot the enclosed.* And it was signed, *The Butcher.* I looked up queryingly.

"But, Homes," I said, "I see nothing of importance here."

"Then you are ready to join the Metropolitan Police and the A.I.C.," he replied acidly. His hand came out to retrieve the note. "The Butcher! That can only be Professor Marty, the most dangerous criminal in all England, and a man who earned the appellation of The Butcher for all too obvious reasons! And you may be sure, Watney, that where Professor Marty is involved, we are dealing with a foe worthy of our mettle!"

"And that little bit of greenish paper that was enclosed?"

"That?" Homes smiled grimly. "Only the answer, I am sure, to the major problem of this entire case—that of their finances!"

"But I do not understand any of this, Homes!" I exclaimed.

"Later," he said, and leaned forward. "Here we are in Bagel Street, and we have much to do if this problem is to be resolved in time."

He thrust a coin at our cabbie and hustled me to the pavement even before our hansom had stopped. I followed him up the stairway to our rooms, to find him already dragging two reference volumes from their shelf; he carried them to the table and turned up the lamp. His next move was to carefully remove the small bit of colored paper from his pocket and place it gently upon the desk top, after which he bent down and began to pore over the opened books, each one page by page. I came to stand beside him, staring down at the small rectangle, and then reached out to pick it up.

"Why, Homes," I exclaimed in disappointment, "it is only a postage stamp. Perforated, I see, and from Ulster Premiums—"

"*Only* a postage stamp, Watney?" He looked at me askance, and then closed the two reference books with a slap. "Do you realize how rare this stamp is? Not only do Stanley Gibbons and Scott fail to list it, but they fail to list any issue marked Premium for any country at all! And pray note the superb mint condition, with the original gum intact, which adds immeasurably to its value! Why, this stamp must be worth a fortune! Five or six of them, released at judicious times on the philatelic market, could easily furnish the funds these miscreants require for their infernal plot."

"But, Homes," I protested, "who could possibly be behind this scheme? Certainly the Professor would not do it out of sheer malice; he must be employed by some group. Who could they possibly be?"

"Ah," said Homes, clasping his hands behind his back and beginning to stride the room. "That is the question! That and, of course, the best way to foil them." He paused a moment, frowning. "As to the people behind this dastardly plot, I am sure the answer lies in that pamphlet, if only I am clever enough to solve it." A grim smile crossed his lips. "As to the best means of stopping these culprits, I believe I already see a rift in that loot." His eyes came up. "Would you do me a favor, Watney?"

"Gladly, Homes," I replied warmly.

"Then I should like you to visit my brother at his club and arrange for me to secure a list of all club stewards in the city of London. And haste, I might mention, is of the essence."

"You may count on me, Homes," I began, but he had already fallen back into his chair and was reaching for the small brochure. It was obvious that he had already forgotten my presence. Pausing only long enough to have lunch, I set about my errand.

It was upon my return, as I was mounting the stairs, that I heard a sharp sound that sent me dashing up the remaining steps to burst through the door. It was only Homes smiting himself on the forehead.

"Of course," he muttered bitterly. "I am a fool! The answer was staring me in the face all along!"

"Homes!" I exclaimed, hurrying forward. "What is it?"

"Look," said he, and pointed a quivering finger at the sheet of paper he had been covering with his calculations. "Note this: if you take the letters in the name 'Professor Marty' and if you eliminate all duplication of letters, you will find you have, respectively, the following: P, R, O, F, E, S, M, A, T, and Y. Placing them in alphabetical order, they then come out: A, E, F, M, O, P, R, S, T, and Y."

He stared at me calculatingly, his eyes bright with excitement. "Now, Watney, if we assign a numerical value to these letters, with A as 1 and Z as 26, then note how they come out!" His fingers hastily marked the numbers down; he looked up triumphantly.

"Watney, they come out 1, 5, 6, 13, 15, 18, 19, 20, and 25!"

"Indubitably, Homes," I agreed doubtfully, and stared at him.

He smiled at my puzzled expression. "Let us now apply these numbers to the pages of this pamphlet," he said gently, "and see what items they refer to." His thin fingers began to turn the pages. "Ah, here we are! Page 1 deals with Upright Pianos; page 5 with Tapestries. Page 6 lists various Hassocks; page 13, Eggbeaters; and page 15, Rotisseries. Page 16 illustrates Ermines; page 18, Bicycles; page 19, Emeralds; page 20 with a variety of Lamps, while page 25 fittingly closes our solution by showing Shovels!"

"Really, Homes," I said worriedly. "You should eat at more regular intervals—"

He waved this aside. *The initials of these items, Watney!* They spell *UP THE REBELS!*" He tossed his quill aside and came to his feet. "I knew that name Sean O'Callahan had a foreign ring! I shall be greatly surprised if, upon investigation, we do not find it to be of Irish origin! I should have realized from the word Ulster that such a possibility existed!"

He nodded his head in conviction. "Think, Watney! To-morrow is the fiftieth anniversary of the Easter Sunday uprising, and what better revenge could they ask than to attack Britain at its most vital spot?—the sanctity of the British club!"

I clasped his hand. "Homes, you have done it again! Only you could have solved the mystery of the brochure in the manner in which you did!" My face fell. "But even knowing this, how are we to stop this vile and despicable scheme?"

"Ah, Watney," he replied, "that is already attended to. You have a list of the stewards?"

"I do," I said with complete honesty, and handed it over.

"Then to work!" said he, and drew from his desk drawer huge sheets of identical stamps. "I shall stuff these into envelopes, and then you shall address them to the list of stewards."

He noted my baffled expression and laughed, albeit ruefully. "A pity, Watney, but there was no other way! While you were visiting Criscroft I was not idle. A friend of mine who is a printer hastily arranged for the printing of these perfect facsimiles."

"But, Homes!" I objected. "If one stamp is so valuable, will not this great number allow them even vaster funds for their foul designs?"

"Ah, Watney," he replied, shaking his head sadly. "It is easily seen that you know nothing of philately. Where one stamp is a great rarity, and worth a fortune, tens of thousands of that same stamp render the entire issue worthless. No, Watney, you may be assured that when these thousands of stamps enter into circulation, the entire scheme will fail!" He patted me on the head and then turned to his desk. "And now to work!"

It was several mornings later that I entered the breakfast room of our quarters, picked up the newspaper, and was just beginning to go through the columns in search of some crime report which might serve as a spring-board to Homes's analytical ability, when my friend came into the room and seated himself opposite me.

"Ah, Watney," said he, spearing a curry, "do you find anything of interest for two idle investigators in your perusal of the news?"

"Very little, Homes," I replied, scanning the leaders. "I do note a case of bankruptcy at some Coupon Trading Company—whatever they are—but such crimes are probably best left to the solicitors."

"I agree," he said, reaching for the cream.

"Although," I added, reading further, "I do note that the president of the company blames his misfortunes on something he calls forgery."

"Forgery?" Homes sat erect. "A dire crime, Watney! And one which no true Englishman will warrant! A note to the authorities offering my services, if you please!"

Postscript:

Criscroft Homes was kind enough to help me prepare this particular adventure for publication, and in the course of proof-reading the cover of the infamous brochure for Ulster Premiums he suddenly paused with a frown.

"I note, Watney," said he, looking up at me, "that further along in this tale you make the statement that only Schlock could have solved this case in the *manner* in which he did."

"That's true," I admitted. "Why?"

He pointed to the booklet cover. "Because," he said, smiling at me proudly, "you were quite correct!"

I am always pleased to be the recipient of a compliment, especially one coming from Criscroft, although in this case I have no idea of why he so flattered me.

Dr. W

ULSTER PREMIUMS

———

Topnotch — Honest — Easy

* * * * *

REDEMPTION EXCHANGE

Battersea Eleven

London, South

✦ ✦ ✦ ✦ ✦ ✦ ✦ ✦ ✦

Editors' Note: We had no more of an eagle-eye than good old Schlock. The acrostic on the brochure cover—the message spelled out by the initials of all the words—slipped past our imperceptive eyes as blithely as they slipped past Schlock's . . . Ah, Watney, we salute your obtuseness; pray move over and hand us the dunce cap. . . .

The Adventure
of the Missing Three-Quarters

My notes for the early part of the year '65 contain several instances of more than passing interest for those who follow the adventures of my friend Mr. Schlock Homes. There was, for example, his brilliant solution to the mysterious gunning down of a retired boilermaker, a case which I find listed as *The Adventure of the Shot and the Bier;* and there is also reference to the intriguing business of the hitchhiking young actress, noted in my journal as *The Adventure of the Ingénue's Thumb.*

It was not, however, until the month of June that a problem of major import came his way, allowing him full scope for his feats of analytical legerdemain, as well as once again permitting him to be of service to his country. In my case-book I find the curious affair noted as *The Adventure of the Missing Three-Quarters.*

It was early afternoon and I had returned to our quarters at 221B Bagel Street; I had been in the midst of a most interesting tracheotomy when I discovered I had somehow forgotten my sutures at home. I went to my room and obtained them, and was passing the sitting-room when I chanced to peer in to find Homes bending absorbedly over his laboratory bench. At the sight of me his face lit up with an excited smile.

"Ah, Watney!" said he with pleasure. "You are just in time! The olives, if you please."

I hastened to comply, and a moment later found myself with a dry martini in my hand and a napkin on my lap. Homes decanted a beaker of the solution into another glass and seated himself across from me. There was a strange look in his eye, a sure sign that this had not been his first laboratory experiment of the day.

"Watney," he said, studying the concoction in his hand, "are you busy this afternoon?"

"Nothing that cannot wait," I replied. "Why do you ask?"

He frowned at his drink for several moments. When at last he spoke, however, it was not to answer my query, but rather to pose a second question of his own.

"Tell me, Watney," he asked slowly, "what do the words 'leg of mutton sleeves,' and 'ruffled hemline,' and 'belt in the back' mean to you?"

I paused, considering his question, and then set my drink aside, tenting my fingers in that pose I had often seen my friend adopt when applying his masterful brain in similar situations.

"Well," I said thoughtfully, "leg of mutton sleeves would undoubtedly be warm, although I should also expect them to be quite greasy. Hemline, of course, is the small village in Germany where the Pied Piper appeared, and after the loss of the children it is scarcely surprising to hear that the village is ruffled. As for belt in the back—" I hesitated a moment and then gave up. "I'm afraid I do not know, Homes," I admitted, "but I must say it sounds a bit cowardly."

To my surprise he did not smile at my failure to define the last phrase. Instead his frown increased and he shook his head.

"To tell you the truth," he said slowly, "I also do not know. However, to satisfy your curiosity regarding these strange words, they were contained in a rather garbled message I received from my brother Criscroft this morning. He further stated that he would drop by after lunch, so possibly we shall soon have clarification." He sat up, his frown disappearing. "Ah! Even sooner than I expected, for here, if I am not mistaken, is Criscroft now."

There was the tramp of footsteps on the stairway; a moment later the door swung back and Criscroft was framed in the opening. He refused my offer of a drink almost curtly, a sure sign of his perturbation, and then flung himself in a chair, regarding the two of us in brooding silence for several moments before he spoke.

"Schlock," he said at last, his voice fraught with worry, "a major crisis has arisen, and I fear I must once again ask your help."

"Of course," Homes said, leaning forward, his eyes warm with sympathy. "How can I be of aid?"

Criscroft continued to frown darkly. "Plans are missing," he said heavily. "Vital plans. If they are not recovered before evening, I fear England shall suffer greatly!"

Homes studied his brother's rigid features and then nodded. "Tell me all."

"Yes." Criscroft came to his feet and began striding the room, his hands clasped tightly behind his back. After several turns up and down he came back to stand before us, staring at the rug fiercely, putting his thoughts in order.

"Yes," he repeated, and brought his eyes up. "Well, the situation is this. As you may or may not know, Britain is suffering gravely from a serious lack of exports, and every means for alleviating the situation has been considered. The Queen's Council on Economic Affairs has determined that priority in the recovery plan shall be given to placing England in first position in the world of fashion." His hand came up abruptly, forestalling interruption. "Do not take the matter lightly! France owes much of its economic strength to women's styles, and we are determined that this rich lode of foreign exchange shall not remain untapped.

"To this end, therefore, the Council has arranged a contest in which designers from every country have been asked to submit their designs. To ensure that fairness prevails, and to reduce the possibility of information leaking out, no sketches or pictures of any kind have been permitted. The designs are being submitted in the form of simple patterns, and the same group of dressmakers—under international supervision— will fabricate all the gowns."

"So far," Homes said with a slight frown, "I see little to disturb you to this degree." His voice became chiding. "Surely you have faith in this country's designers being easily able to dominate a contest of this—or any other—sort?"

"You do not know the whole unhappy story. Pray allow me to continue. Well, we selected as our entrant a most promising young talent. His name is Donald Orr—head of D. Orr & Company—and in order to free him completely from other preoccupations during the contest, we arranged for him to do his work

63

at Medicinal Manor, the town home of the Earl of Wintergreen. He—" Criscroft paused and eyed Homes sharply. "You spoke?"

"No, no. It is only that I am familiar with Medicinal Manor; the Earl is an old friend of mine. I have been fortunate enough to enjoy the cuisine there several times; Jenny, his cook, is undoubtedly the finest in all London. But I digress—pray forgive me, and continue."

"Ah! Well, possibly your knowledge of the premises will be of some usefulness. We shall see. To go on, then: Orr completed his work early this morning and then hid his patterns before he left the Manor for a brief walk. Unfortunately, he has spent some time recently in the American colonies, and he apparently forgot his 'Look Right, Look Left,' because when he stepped from a kerb on his way back, he was struck by a dray, and even now is in St. Barts in bad state."

I sat up in alarm. "If I can be of any assistance—"

"No, no! He is in competent hands; a nurse's aide is caring for him. The thing is, he is unconscious, and the only words he spoke before he lapsed into his unconscious condition was to say he had hidden the plans in the kitchen. Those phrases I sent you this morning were found on a slip of paper in his pocket. Needless to say, we have searched the culinary area thoroughly, but without success. The Earl was not informed of the purpose of Orr's visit, and therefore can be of no aid. Frankly, unless you can help, we are lost!"

Criscroft's voice sank even lower.

"The contest ends to-night, and the dressmakers will work until dawn in order to present the gowns early to-morrow morning. If we are unable to locate the patterns by six o'clock this evening, England will have initiated a contest in which it will not even have an entrant! You can easily imagine the shame of it!"

Homes peaked his fingers and closed his eyes as he considered the complex problem. At last he opened them, looking up and speaking thoughtfully.

"To attempt to solve the code contained in those garbled phrases," said he, "would undoubtedly take more time than we have at our disposal. No; our only hope is to once again search the kitchen at the Manor, but this time to do it with more intelligence." He came to his feet swiftly. "If you will allow me time to dress suitably, I shall join you at once."

Criscroft shook his head sadly. "Much as I should like to accompany you, and vital as this case is, I fear it cannot be. To-day is our weekly whist at the club." His eyes came up, stern and demanding. "But remember this, Schlock—England's future is in your hands!"

"I shall not forget!" Homes promised in a ringing voice, and then swung about, perplexed. "Now, what was I looking for a minute ago? Ah, yes. My deerstalker!"

It was less than an hour later that our hansom cab deposited us at the door of Medicinal Manor in Payne Square. Homes paid the cabby and we mounted the steps; the pull-cord was finally answered by Rhett, the old butler. His wizened face broke into a smile of delight as he recognized my companion.

"Mr. Homes, sir! It's good to see you again! Come in, come in."

"Hello, Rhett," Homes said genially, and followed the bent figure into the cavernous hallway, with me close at his heels. "Is your master at home?"

The old retainer's smile disappeared as he closed the door and turned to face us. He shook his head sadly. "I'm afraid not, Mr. Homes. He has taken the children off for the day, to take their minds from the troubles, poor tykes. I fear you have come at a bad time, sir."

"Troubles? Bad time?" Homes inquired sharply. "How is that?"

Old Rhett spread his veined hands apologetically. "Well, sir, first there was that tragic affair of that young gentleman, Mr. Orr, going out and stepping beneath a horse, and shortly thereafter Jenny went sneaking from the kitchen with something under her apron—undoubtedly food—and locked herself in her room, refusing to open the door."

Homes frowned. "Jenny? Locked herself in her room?"

"Yes, sir. Undoubtedly a fit of temper caused by too many guests. However, I have been given instructions by the gentlemen from the Home Office to give you the run of the house, so—" His gnarled hand waved gently towards the interior of the house. "If you require me for anything, sir, you have only to ring."

"Thank you, Rhett," Homes said in a kindly voice, and led me in the direction of the kitchen. On our way he paused a moment outside of the cook's room, but the only sound to be heard from within was a faint whirring, as of some kind of machine. With a shrug at the inexplicable sounds made by women in a temper, Homes continued down the passage.

The vast kitchen was strangely empty without the

presence of Jenny, and Homes stared about silently for several moments, his sharp eyes taking in the two huge wood ranges, the ice-chest, as well as the coffee-grinder in one corner.

"Well, Watney," he said thoughtfully at last, "we have little time. We had best get right to it."

He began his search with the ovens, and then considered the other modern appliances; all proved empty of anything useful to his purpose. He then attacked the cupboards, going through them carefully, after which he moved to the drawers. Each was withdrawn, peered into intently, and then replaced. The closets followed, and when these had also been inspected without yielding any clew, Homes stepped back, frowning blackly.

"If Mr. Orr said he hid them in the kitchen," he muttered, almost to himself, "then he hid them in the kitchen! He would have no reason to lie. We must be overlooking something."

"But what, Homes?" I asked in bewilderment.

"I do not know!" he replied savagely, and then bent, as a last resort, to look beneath the sink. The rubbish bin there was filled to capacity; there was a sudden startled gasp from my companion, and then he swiftly reached out to pick something from the top of the bin. He arose with a strange light in his eye. I moved closer; he was holding a plain card-board tube about twelve inches in length and approximately one inch in diameter.

"But, Homes!" I cried. "What is it? Why are you studying it so intently?"

"Later, Watney," he exclaimed, and in two strides had returned to the cupboard counter, staring down at it with a gleam in his eye. I followed his glance, but all I could note were some crumbs and a knife lying back against a bread-board. Homes was nodding to himself in satisfaction; his whole attitude clearly demonstrated that he had discovered some valuable clew overlooked by the previous searchers.

"Of course!" he muttered to himself. "I am a fool! I should have seen it at once!"

"Seen what, Homes?" I asked, puzzled by the entire affair.

"There is no time now," he said, turning to me swiftly. "Ring for the butler at once."

Completely mystified, I hastened to follow his orders, and a moment later old Rhett had shuffled into the room. Homes moved forward, his eyes gleaming. "You say his Lordship has taken the children off for the afternoon. Did he perchance take them for a picnic tea in Hempstead Heath?"

"Why, yes, Mr. Homes," said the butler in utter amazement, "although how you knew it, I cannot imagine!"

"No matter," Homes said in triumph, and leaned closer. "What part of the heath would he be most likely to visit? Come, man, think! Time is of the essence!"

"His Lordship usually favors the Poet's Corner—" Rhett began in his quavering voice, but Homes had already disengaged himself and was moving quickly and purposefully towards the front of the house.

He trotted rapidly down the steps with me at his heels and flagged down the first hansom that appeared, jumping into it and pulling me after. "Hempstead Heath, driver!" he cried urgently. "The Poet's Corner! And hurry!"

68

We came clattering up through Swiss Cottage in the direction of Golder's Green while I hung on desperately to the sides of the swaying vehicle and tried to make sense out of what was happening. Homes was leaning forward eagerly, his hair whipping about his face, as if in this way to somehow hasten our passage. The mysterious card-board tube was clutched fiercely in one hand.

"Homes!" I cried. "Pray explain! This whole thing is completely confusing."

"Is it?" he asked over his shoulder, and then leaned back, coming into the greater protection of the cab. He turned to me with a wide smile on his face. "We have ample time before we arrive at the heath, so allow me to give you a brief lesson in logic."

He raised the card-board tube, using it to tick off his points against the fingers of his other hand.

"One: we know the patterns were hidden in the kitchen. Two: they are not there now. The only possible conclusion to be reached is that they have been removed. But, excepting for the children, only two people have left the house—Mr. Donald Orr and his Lordship. Certainly there is no reason to suspect Mr. Orr, which only leaves us his Lordship. Therefore it was he who removed them."

I sat up in alarm. "The Earl of Wintergreen a traitor?"

"No, no, Watney! Remember that his Lordship was not familiar with the purpose of Mr. Orr's presence in his home, nor of the contest. True, he removed the patterns, but he did it inadvertently."

"Inadvertently?" I exclaimed.

"Precisely! You may recall the crumbs on the cupboard counter. Certainly Jenny, before locking herself in her room for some unknown reason, would not have left her kitchen in such a state of disarray. She is far too well-trained for that. Therefore, somebody used it after her. Since it could only have been his Lordship, and since he was taking the children out, it was fairly easy to deduce a picnic tea. Hempstead Heath being the closest park, it was logical to assume he had taken them there."

I shook my head in admiration. "It is so clear when you explain it, Homes." I said, and then frowned. "But you have still said nothing of the missing patterns."

He raised the thin card-board tube he had been holding so tightly. "This, Watney, is an empty container for a roll of waxed paper. When his Lordship discovered he was out of waxed paper in which to wrap his sandwiches, he quite naturally searched for a substitute, and found the patterns. Being unaware of their true importance—"

I stared at him, aghast. "Homes! You mean?—"

"Exactly! Let us pray we are not too late!" He bent forward again as our cab swerved wildly into the heath and raced along the winding dirt road that led to the Poet's Corner. Suddenly Homes raised himself, peering forward excitedly. "That carriage!" he cried. "It is Wintergreen's—he is leaving!"

Our driver leaned down from his box, shouting tensely. The spirit of the chase had undoubtedly entered him as well. "Shall I go after him, sir?"

"No, no!" Homes cried. "Stop here! And wait for us!" He flung a coin in the direction of our jehu and dragged me from the cab even before it had fully stopped. "Watney! Quickly, before the wind snatches them away! The sandwich-wrappers!"

We rushed about, picking up the pieces of paper and smoothing them out, attempting to get them all, and then at last paused, panting, when the last visible one had been rescued. Homes's sharp eyes scanned the landscape, but as far as we could see, none of the wrappers had escaped us. With the precious pieces of paper held tightly, my friend ran back to the hansom and entered. I climbed wearily in behind him and fell against the seat, fighting for my breath. The driver instantly whipped up his horses, heading for the City.

"And now, Homes?" I asked, when at last I was able to speak.

"Now?" he responded, leaning back with a triumphant smile on his face. "Now we shall deliver these patterns to Criscroft at his club, after which our obligation will have been fulfilled. It has been a pretty problem, and I believe this evening I shall relax from it with a few bars of Hershey on my violin. If you wish you may turn the pages."

"I should like that, Homes," I exclaimed warmly, "but I really do think I should return to the hospital. The chap I left there this morning has been remarkably patient, but still—"

It was well past the hour of noon when, exhausted by our efforts of the previous day, I entered the breakfast room to find Homes already there before me, the afternoon newspaper at his elbow, attacking his first kipper with Vigor, a new sauce he found to his liking.

At the sight of me he glanced up from his journal, and then nodded as he answered the unspoken question in my eyes.

"Yes, Watney," he said gently, with a smile on his lips. "Our efforts of yesterday were crowned with success. Look for yourself."

He reached across the table, placing the folded journal on my plate; I seated myself and drew it to me. There was a picture on the front page; the headline above it read: *ENGLAND WINS FASHION CONTEST,* while below it, in smaller letters, was the caption: *Miniskirt Is Born!*

I frowned in puzzlement at the strange words, glanced at the picture, and then raised dazed eyes to my companion.

"Homes! Do you suppose—?"

He returned my horrified look equably. "It did occur to me last evening that possibly the Earl and the children had not eaten all their sandwiches, but had taken some home. However"—he shrugged—"one should never quarrel with success." His smile dismissed the discussion. "And now, Watney, since you have the journal in hand, what other news do you find that might be of interest to us?"

I glanced at the prize-winning costume once again, and then hastily turned the page, running my eye down the columns, searching. Suddenly my eyebrows shot up.

"Homes!" I exclaimed. "Indeed there is! His Lordship, the Earl of Wintergreen, has asked assistance in locating his missing cook!"

Homes sat up in alarm. "Jenny has disappeared?"

"Yes," I said, and read further into the article. "It

72

says here that when last seen, she was wearing a dress with puffed sleeves, a pleated skirt, and with a sash behind."

"With that description there should be no trouble in locating her," Homes said thoughtfully, and laid aside his napkin. "A telegram to his Lordship offering my services, if you will, Watney!"

The Adventure
of the Disappearance
# of Whistler's Mother

It was seldom, indeed, that the successful conclusion of a case left my friend Mr. Schlock Homes dissatisfied and unhappy; but one such affair did occur in the latter part of '66, and I relate the case to demonstrate how the best intentions of the finest of men can at times lead to unwanted results.

The months preceding this particular affair had been busy ones, and reference to my case-book for that period reveals numerous examples in which his analytical genius was given full opportunity for expression. There was, for example, his brilliant solution to the strange affair of the American baseball manager who went berserk, which I find noted as *The Adventure of the Twisted Lip;* and shortly thereafter his attention was drawn to the mysterious curse placed upon the south forty of a local grange owned by a prominent manufacturer of stomach drugs. I am sure my readers will recognize the case, which I later delineated as *The Adventure of the Bane in the Lower Tract.*

One might reasonably have imagined, this being so, that when at long last a dropping off of activity afforded my friend a well-needed chance for rest he would have been pleased; but such was not the case.

Boredom was always distasteful to Homes, and I was not surprised, therefore, to return to our quarters at 221B Bagel Street one late, blustery afternoon in October to find my friend, hands thrust deep into the pockets of his dressing-gown, sprawled out in a chair before the fireplace, glowering fiercely into the flames.

Nor did he greet me in his customary manner, but came to his feet at my entrance and moved to the window restlessly, scowling down at the pavement.

I set aside my bag, removed my greatcoat and bowler, and was just turning to the sideboard when a sharp ejaculation caused me to swing about and contemplate Homes. He was leaning forward, staring down at the street in sudden excitement, his entire attitude expressing inordinate interest.

"Homes!" I exclaimed. "What is it?"

"Come here, Watney," said he, and drew the curtains further apart as I obediently hurried to his side. His thin finger pointed downward, quivering with excitement. "What do you make of that poor fellow there? Harrowed, is he not?"

My glance followed the direction of his finger. The figure to which Homes was referring was dashing madly from one side of the street to the other, studying the numerals of the houses in obvious agitation. Despite the dank chill of the day he wore neither cape nor beaver; his hair was tousled, his weskit awry, and his manner extremely disturbed.

"Harrowed?" I repeated wonderingly, watching the eccentric path woven by the man below. "In my opinion, medically speaking, he appears not so much harrowed as ploughed."

"No matter," Homes replied with barely concealed triumph. "The important fact is that he is coming to visit us, for you will note he has paused before our doorstep, and even now is entering. And here, if I am not mistaken, is our visitor now."

Homes was, as usual, correct, for there was the sound of footsteps pounding loudly on the stairs, and a moment later the door burst open. The disheveled man stood panting upon the threshold, casting his eyes about wildly until they lit on Homes.

"Schlock 'Omes!" he cried in a thick French accent. "Thank *le bon Dieu* I 'ave found you in!"

At closer sight of our visitor, Homes's eyes widened in sudden recognition. He hurried forward, taking our perturbed guest by the arm and leading him to an easy chair beside the fireplace.

"Duping!" he cried. "My Lord, man, what is the trouble? What brings you to London? And in this sorry state?" He turned to me, his eyes glowing. "Watney, this is none other than my old friend from Paris, Monsieur C. Septembre Duping! You may recall that back in '41 I was able to be of some slight assistance to him in that sinister business of the simian with the inclination for strangling women and stuffing them up chimneys."

"Of course," I replied warmly, my eyes fixed upon our famous visitor with admiration. "As I recall, I even recorded the case in my notes as *The Adventure of the Monk's Habit.*"

"Precisely," Homes agreed, and swung back to our guest, dropping into a chair across from him and leaning forward sympathetically. "Septembre, pray tell us what is bothering you."

The man seated facing him took a deep breath and then nodded. The warmth of the room after the raw weather outdoors had obviously done much to relax him, as well as the fact that I had hastened to furnish him with a whisky, taking one myself to keep him company.

"Yais," he said heavily, and raised troubled eyes to my friend's face. " 'Omes, a terrible thing 'as 'appened. I know you are too *occupé* to come to Paris, but I still wished for ze benefit of your analytical brain."

"Of course," Homes replied warmly. "What is the problem?"

Our guest laid aside his empty glass and hesitated a moment, as if to emphasize the extreme gravity of the matter. When at last he spoke, the very quietness of his tone impressed us with his seriousness. " 'Omes, he said slowly, *"Whistler's Mother 'as been stolen!"*

If he had expected any great reaction from Homes, he was surely disappointed, for other than a slight narrowing of his eyes, caused by a puff of smoke from the fireplace, my friend's face remained impassive. "Ah? Most interesting. Pray continue."

"Yais." Duping sighed deeply and then plunged ahead. "Well, ze facts are zese. *Hier,* at ze Louvre, zey 'ave a *réception* for a new painter 'oo is visiting Paris, and to make ze affair properly impressive, zey arrange it in ze form of a musical *soirée,* calling ze program ' 'Ello, Dali.' I mention zis fact only to explain why zere was so unusual-large a crowd zere; how you say, *normalment* at zis hour ze Louvre is quite empty. Well, to make a long story *court,* at nine o'clock, when ze *musicale* is start, Whistler's Mother is zere, where she 'as been for years. At ten o'clock, when everybody leave—'' He spread his hands. "Gone! Wizout a clew!"

Homes, nodded, his eyes fixed on the other's unhappy expression. "I see."

"Yais. Well, I imagine you will want ze description." Our visitor thought a moment, assembling the data in his mind, and then continued. "A black background, and gray. 'Er size, in your English measurements, *approximativement* five-foot-four by four-foot-nine. As you can well understand, a 'eavy frame, of course. What else? Ah, yais—ze age. About ninety-five years, I believe." He shook his head sadly. "Let us 'ope she is in good condition when returned, and not damaged or smashed."

Homes nodded and sprang to his feet, beginning to pace the room, his thin hands clasped tightly behind his back. After several turns he came to stand before our guest, staring down with a frown on his face. "And has a reward been offered?"

Duping shrugged. "Money is no object, 'Omes. We will pay anyzing for ze return." He also rose, moving in the direction of the doorway. "We 'ave ze suspicion zat Whistler's Mother may already 'ave been smuggled out of France, possibly 'ere to England."

"A natural conclusion," Homes agreed. "And where are you staying in London?"

"I do not stay. I return at once to Paris. I came only to ask your 'elp."

"And you shall have it! You may expect to hear from me quite soon, giving you my solution to this puzzle. I shall get right to it this very evening, my dear Septembre."

"But, 'Omes—I mean, Homes," I interrupted in

disappointment. "You have forgotten. We have tickets for Albert Hall to-night. The Rome Flood-Control Chorus is doing 'Hold That Tiber.' "

He waved aside my objection almost impatiently. "Duty before pleasure, Watney," he replied a bit coldly. "Besides, I am not particularly interested in a program consisting solely of popular tunes."

"But there is also classical music," I insisted, a bit stung by his tone. "Cyd Caesar is completing the program by playing the 'Etude Brutus.' "

Homes thought a moment and then shook his head. "In that case it is a pity, but I have already given my word." He returned his attention to our guest. "One last question, Septembre," he said softly, staring at the other intently. "And once the return is effected—?"

"We shall 'ang 'er, of course," Duping replied simply, and closed the door behind him.

No sooner had our guest left than Homes flung himself back into his chair, tenting his fingers, and staring across them towards me with a dark frown on his hawk-like features.

"A tragedy, is it not, Watney?"

"Indeed it is," I readily agreed. "An old woman kidnapped!"

"No, no!" He shook his head at me impatiently. "You missed the entire point! The tragedy is that a poor wine-stewardess in a night-club should face such a penalty for the mere pilfering of several bottles of wine. Particularly since the poor soul was under the influence at the time and scarcely liable for her actions."

"I beg your pardon?" I asked bewildered. "I heard nothing to-day of night-clubs or wine-stewardesses. In fact, with the small amount of information Monsieur Duping furnished, I do not see how you can possibly hope to come up with any answer to the puzzle."

"Small amount of information? Really, Watney, at times I despair of you! Duping gave us more information than we really needed. For example, there was his description of the woman. Obviously, if she is five-foot-four by four-foot-nine, there was no need to inform us that she has a heavy frame. Similarly, if they plan to hang her when and if they get her back, it was scarcely necessary to tell us that her background was black. And being ninety-five years of age, one could automatically assume she would be gray. No, no, Watney! Duping gave us all we require. The real problem is how to handle it."

He swung about and stared fiercely into the flames of the fireplace, speaking almost as if to himself.

"There is a possibility, of course, that we can not only satisfy Duping but still save the poor old lady's life. If only—" He nodded to himself several times, and then turned around to face the room, glancing at his time-piece. "A bit early to make our move, though."

"Really, Homes," I said, deeply annoyed. "I honestly believe you are pulling my leg. That business before of wine-stewardesses and night-clubs! And now this mysterious muttering you are indulging in! What move, pray, is it too early to make?"

"Why," Homes replied, surprised, "to break into Professor Marty's digs, of course." He noted the

80

expression on my face and suddenly smiled in a kindly fashion. "No, Watney, I am not teasing you. We have at least an hour to spare, so let me explain this sad case to you."

He leaned in my direction, ticking his points off methodically on his fingers.

"Let us start with Duping's description of the place where the old lady was last seen and from which she disappeared, this place called the Louvre—or, in English, The Louver. That the place is a night-club is instantly discernible: the fact that normally it was deserted between the hours of nine and ten, long before the most frivolous of French patrons would think of beginning their evening's entertainment, the presence of music in the form of this 'Hello, Dali' revue; and most important, the name, so typical, and so similar to The Venetian Blind or The Window or The Cellar or others which we know to be so popular in Soho to-day. I should not hesitate to predict that its decor consists of louvers painted in green against a puce background. But no matter—let us continue."

A second finger was bent over to join the first, while I listened in open-mouthed wonder to his brilliant deductions.

"Now, precisely what was this elderly lady doing in this night-club? Obviously, she was not merely an habituée. Duping's exact words were, 'Where she 'as been for years.' Had she been a client, even the most constant, he almost certainly would have worded it differently. He would have said, 'Where she 'as been in ze 'abit of dropping in for years,' or something of that nature. Therefore, not being a client, we are

81

forced to the conclusion that she is—or was, rather—
an employee of the establishment, and one of long
standing, at that.

"But in what position?" He shrugged before continuing. "Well, considering her age and her measurements, I believe we can safely eliminate the positions
of waitress and hat-check girl, both of which demand
a certain degree of beauty. Matron in the Mesdames?
Again, I believe we can disregard this possibility; her
exact presence or absence at any particular hour
would scarcely have been noted with the exactitude
that Duping indicated. And the same holds true, of
course, for any of the kitchen staff. Cashier? With her
black background it is doubtful if the owners would
permit her near the till. There is, therefore, only one
position left: Mrs. Whistler could only have been the
wine-stewardess!"

A third finger was depressed as I listened, amazed,
to this startling demonstration of incontrovertible
logic. Homes's eyes remained half-closed as he continued to clothe the thin facts given by his friend with
the warm flesh of his impeccable analysis.

"Now, Watney, consider: How could an old lady like
this manage to subject herself to a penalty as severe
as hanging in the short period allowed her between
the hours of nine and ten? Certainly her crime was not
murder, for which the French still maintain the guillo-
tine. It must therefore have been something equally
severe in the eyes of her accusers, but short of murder.
It must also, of necessity, be something within her
power to perform. Recalling that her position was that
of a wine-stewardess, and that she had no access to any
of the funds of the club, we can only reach one conclu-

sion: that her crime consisted of taking some of the wine stocks. Undoubtedly rare and precious, and therefore probably cognac."

"But, Homes!" I objected. "Hanging? Just for stealing a few bottles of wine?"

He smiled at me pityingly. "It is apparent you know little of human nature, Watney. In the American colonies, as I am sure you are aware, the penalty for stealing a horse is hanging. And not so long ago punishment even more severe was reserved for anyone taking the King's deer. Why should France, where their national pride in their liqueurs is paramount, feel any less strongly? No, no! It is the only conclusion consistent with all the facts, and therefore must be the correct one. You know my dictum: when all theories but one have been eliminated, that remaining theory, however improbable—indeed, however impossible—must be the truth—or words to that effect."

I nodded dumbly. "Now," Homes went on, "when Duping told us that she had been stolen, you assumed his poor English prevented him from using the word 'kidnapped.' Actually, his poor English prevented him from stating what he truly meant—not that she had been stolen, but that she herself had stolen something."

I could not help but accept the faultless conclusion. "But, Homes," I said hopefully, "you suggest there were mitigating circumstances?"

"Yes. As I have already said, the poor woman was obviously under the influence of alcohol. You may recall Duping stating that he hoped she would not be 'smashed' when apprehended. It is an American slang term apparently becoming popular even in France. In any event, his very fear of this indicates that she stole the bottles in order to drink them—proof positive that her excessive thirst caused her crime in the first place. That she chose a moment when everyone was concentrating on the revue is easily understood. Under normal conditions she would have been too busy serving customers to have succumbed to the temptation to imbibe."

"But you say you hope to be able not only to satisfy Duping but also save the old lady?"

"There is that possibility."

"And this somehow involves Professor Marty?"

"Exactly." He considered me sombrely. "It will mean a bit of a risk to-night, but there is nothing else for it. If you do not care to join me in this venture, I shall not hold it against you. The Professor is undoubtedly the most dangerous man in all England."

"Nothing on earth could stop me from accompanying you, Homes!" I declared stoutly, and then frowned. "But where does Professor Marty come into this at all?"

He shook his head impatiently at my lack of perception. "Please, Watney! You may recall that when Duping suggested the old lady might even now be in England, I readily agreed. Why? Because the name Whistler is certainly not French, but rather British, and in times of trouble to whom would she turn, if not to her son in England? We can scarcely believe that with her black background her son is free of a taint of malfeasance, and no criminal in England is beyond the scope of knowledge of Professor Marty. No, no! If Whistler's mother is in England at the moment, you may be sure the Professor is well aware of it. By entering his rooms after he has left on his nightly foray against society, I hope to find proof of the fact. And possibly turn it to the advantage of the poor soul!"

"Bravo, Homes!" I cried, and could not help applauding both his motives and his infallible logic. Unfortunately, at the moment I was holding both a glass and a bottle, and while I shame-facedly hastened to clear up the debris, Homes disappeared into his room to change into more suitable raiment.

It was past the hour of ten when our hansom dropped us around the corner of Professor Marty's darkened rooms in Limehouse. The night had turned cold, which afforded us a good excuse to keep our collars high and our faces hidden from the denizens of the district, who slunk past us to fade into the growing miasma rising from the river beyond. With a glance in both directions, Homes chose a moment when a swirl of fog momentarily hid us from any passers-by to swiftly mount the steps and apply his skill to the lock. A moment later he was beckoning me to follow; scant seconds more and he had closed the door, and his bull's-eye lantern was casting its restricted beam about the empty room.

"Quickly, Watney!" he whispered urgently. "We have little time! You take the den and the bedroom, while I examine the kitchen and bath." He took one look at my opening lips and added coldly, "We are looking for anything that might indicate the presence of the old lady here."

I nodded and began to close my mouth when I remembered something else. "But I have no lantern, Homes."

"Use vestas, then, if need be, but hurry!"

He disappeared even as I was fumbling beneath my cape, and an eerie chill swept over me until I had the first one lit and spied a taper on the mantel-piece. A moment later I was shielding the flickering flame and studying the room in which I stood. To me it appeared as any other room, and my heart sank as I realized how ill-equipped I was for a search of this nature, and that I might very well fail my friend. To bolster my spirits I went to the liquor cabinet, and at that moment the beam of Homes's lantern joined my weaker candle as he returned to the den.

"There is nothing," he said in a dispirited voice, and then his tone sharpened. "Watney! What are you doing?"

"Nothing—" I began guiltily, but before I could offer my excuses he had dropped down beside me and was reaching past my arm for the contents of the cabinet. A moment later and he was pounding my back in congratulation.

"Watney, you have done it! Good man!"

I stared in bewilderment as he began withdrawing bottles and examining them, muttering half to himself as he did so. "Cordon Bleu, Remy Martin, Napoleon, Courvoisier—excellent! With any luck this should do it!"

"But, Homes!" I interjected. "I do not understand. Do what?"

He swung to me with a fierce light of triumph in his eyes. "My dear Watney! When Duping expressed fear that the old lady would be apprehended in an inebriated state, he was not worrying about *her,* since he gave no indication of reducing the penalty for her crime. No, he was fearful that the cognacs would be consumed, for they are his main interest. By returning these to him, it is well possible that he will allow the matter to drop, and stop his pursuit of the poor woman."

His eyes swung about the room. "Quickly! Find me something in which to package these bottles while I pen a brief note to Duping to enclose. The packet to Le Havre leaves on the midnight tide, and by hurrying we can just make it."

While he bent over the escritoire, I hastily searched the room for wrapping materials, but despite my efforts the best I could find was an old roll of canvas that had been shoved behind a bookcase. I brought it forward hesitatingly and showed it to Homes.

"Ah, well," he said, shrugging, "it is certainly not the cleanest, for somebody has smeared it with tar or something. However, we have no time for further delays—it will have to do. Help me roll these bottles in it and we will be on our way to the dock. With any luck these will be in Duping's hands to-morrow, and our problem will have been solved."

Our exertions of the previous evening kept us both late abed, and it was close to the hour of noon before I came into our breakfast room to find Homes already at the table. He nodded to me pleasantly and was about to speak when our page entered and handed Homes a telegraph form.

I seated myself, unfolded the afternoon journal, and was just reaching for the curried kidney when a sharp exclamation of dismay caused me to glance up. Homes, his face ashen, was staring in horror at the slip of paper in his hand.

"Homes!" I cried. "What is it?"

"I am an idiot!" he muttered bitterly. "An abysmal idiot! I should have anticipated this!"

"Anticipated what, Homes?" I inquired, and for an answer received the telegraph form flung across the table. I read it hastily; its message was succinct. HOMES, YOU HAVE DONE IT AGAIN. WHISTLER'S MOTHER IS ONCE AGAIN IN OUR HANDS AND HUNG, THANKS TO YOU.

"But, Homes!" I exclaimed. "I do not understand!"

"No?" he replied scathingly. "It is easily enough understood. I failed to take into account that the old lady might follow her booty back across the channel and thus fall into their hands! I am a fool! Rather than save her, I actually led her to her death."

"You must not blame yourself, Homes," I said with warm sympathy. "You did your best, and no man can do more."

"I did far too well," he replied balefully. "Without my help Duping might have searched for the old woman and her cognac for years." He tried to shake off his black mood, shrugging. "Ah, well! It is too late now to cry over spilt milk. Tell me, Watney, is there anything of a criminal nature in to-day's journal to help take my mind from this terrible fiasco?"

I hastily abandoned my kidney, perusing the newspaper instead, running my eyes rapidly down one column after another, but without too much success. There was, however, one weak possibility, and in lieu of a more interesting case I offered it.

"There is this, Homes," I said, studying the article further. "It seems that a very valuable painting was stolen from the French National Gallery. But the date-line is several days old; it may very well be that by this time the trail is much too cold."

The renewed sparkle in Homes's eyes told me that he was already well on the road to recovery.

"The time element makes no difference, Watney! A crime is a crime, and the more difficult the case, the better I like it! Besides, we have one bit of information the Sûreté lacks: we know that Professor Marty could not have been involved, for we would have come upon some evidence of it during our search. And eliminating this adversary takes us quite a step forward! A telegram to the authorities offering my services, Watney, if you will!"

The Adventure of the Dog in the Knight

In glancing through my notebook delineating the many odd adventures which I was fortunate enough to share with my good friend Mr. Schlock Homes in the early months of the year '68, I find it difficult to select any single one as being truly indicative of his profound ability to apply his personal type of analytical *Verwirrung* which, taken at its ebb, so often led him on to success.

There was, of course, the case of the nefarious card-cheat whom Homes so cleverly unmasked in a young men's health organization in the small village of Downtree in Harts—a case I find noted in my journal as *The Adventure of the Y-Bridge.* It is also true that during this period he was of particular assistance to the British Association of Morticians in a case whose details are buried somewhere in my files but which resulted, as I recall, in a National Day being set aside in their honor. While it remains a relatively unimportant matter, the tale still is recorded in my case-book as *The Boxing-Day Affair.*

However, in general those early months were fruitless, and it was not until the second quarter of the year that a case of truly significant merit drew his attention. In my entry for the period of 15/16 April, '68, I find the case listed as *The Adventure of the Dog in the Knight.*

It had been an unpleasantly damp day with a drizzle compounded by a miasmic fog that kept us sequestered in our quarters at 221B Bagel Street; but evening brought relief in the form of a brisk breeze that quickly cleared the heavy air. "We have been in too long," Homes said, eyeing me queryingly. "I suggest a walk to clear away the cobwebs."

I was more than willing. Homes had spent his day at the laboratory bench, and between the stench of his chemicals and the acrid odor of the Pakistanis, the room fairly reeked. For several hours we roamed the by-ways of our beloved London, our coat-collars high against the evening chill, stopping on occasion at various pubs to ascertain the hour. It was eight o'clock exactly when we arrived back at our rooms, and it was to find a hansom cab standing at the kerb before our door.

"Ah," Homes observed, eyeing the conveyance sharply. "A visitor from Scotland Yard, I see!"

I was sufficiently conversant with Homes's methods by this time to readily follow his reasoning; for the crest of the Yard—three feet rampant on a field of corn—was emblazoned both on the door and on the rear panel of the coach, clearly visible under the gaslamp before our house, and the jehu sitting patiently on the box was both uniformed and helmeted. With some curiosity as to the reason for this late visit I followed Homes up the stairs and into our quarters.

A familiar figure rose from a chair beside the unlit fireplace and turned to face us. It was none other than Inspector Balustrade, an old antagonist whose overbearing manner and pompous posturing had long grated upon both Homes's nerves and my own. Before we could even discard our outer garments he was speaking in his usual truculent manner.

"My advice to you, Homes," he said a bit threateningly, "is to keep your hands off the Caudal Hall affair. We have an open-and-shut case, and any interference on your part can only cause the luckless miscreant unwarranted and futile hope. In fact," he continued, looking fiercer than ever, "I believe I shall go so far as to *demand* that you leave the matter alone!"

Schlock Homes was quite the wrong person to address in such words and tones. "Inspector Balustrade, do not rail at me!" said he sharply. He doffed his coat and deerstalker, tossing them carelessly upon a chair, striding forward to face the Inspector. "I take those cases that interest me, and it is my decision alone that determines which they shall be."

"Ah!" Inspector Balustrade's tiny eyes lit up in self-congratulation. "I knew it—I knew it! I merely wished to confirm my suspicions. So they've been at you, eh? And, by the look of things, bought you! Lock, Stock, and Barrel!"

"Eh?"

"The lawyer chappies, that is," Balustrade continued. "Well, you're wasting your time listening to them, Mr. Homes. There is no doubt of the culprit's guilt." He smiled, a sneering smile. "Or do you honestly believe you have sufficient evidence to contradict that statement?"

"What I think is my affair," Homes said, eyeing the man distastefully. "You have delivered your message, Inspector, so I see little to be gained by your continued presence here."

"As you wish, Mr. Homes," Balustrade said with mock servility. He picked up his ulster, clamped his bowler firmly to his head, and moved to the door. "But Dr. Watney here can bear witness that I did my best to save you from making a fool of yourself!" And with a chuckle he disappeared down the stairs.

"Homes!" I said chidingly. "A new case and you did not inform me?"

"Believe me," he said sincerely, "I know nothing of this. I have no idea what the Inspector was talking of." He contemplated me with a frown. "Is it possible, Watney, that we have inadvertently missed some item of importance in the morning journal?"

"It would be most unusual, Homes," I began, and then suddenly remembered something. "I do recall, now, Mrs. Essex borrowing the front page of the *Globe* to wrap some boots for the cobbler's boy to pick up, but if I'm not mistaken, the lad failed to appear. Let me get it and see if it can cast any light on this mystery."

I hurried into the scullery, returning in moments with the missing sheet. I spread it open upon the table, pressing out the creases, while Homes came to stand at my side.

"Ah," said he, pointing triumphantly. "There it is!" He bent closer, reading the words half-aloud. *"Tragic Affair at Caudal Manor.* But where is the—? Ah, here it is just beneath the headline." He smiled in satisfaction at his discovery, and read on:

" 'Late last evening an unfortunate incident occurred at Caudal Manor, the country estate in Kent of Sir Francis Gibbon, the 62-year-old Knight of the Realm. A small dinner party was in progress, at which the only guests were Sir Francis' sister-in-law, Mrs.

Gabriel Gibbon, who is married to Sir Francis' younger and only brother and who has often acted as hostess for her bachelor brother-in-law; and a Mr. John Wain, a young visitor from the Colony of California, a chemist by trade, who is staying with Mr. and Mrs. Gabriel Gibbon as a house-guest. Mr. Gabriel, two years younger than his illustrious brother, was absent, having claimed he preferred to see his romance at the theatre rather than at home, and for this reason was spending his evening at the latest Boucicault offering in Piccadilly. Readers of the society news may recall that the beauteous Mrs. Gibbon, like Mr. Wain, was also a colonial from California at the time of her marriage two years ago.

" 'The main course, chosen out of deference to their foreign guest, was frankfurters—called "hot-dogs" abroad—which was also a favorite dish of his Lordship, Sir Francis. This course had already been consumed, washed down with ale, and a bitter-almond tart had also been eaten, when Sir Francis suddenly gasped, turned pale, and seemed to be having difficulty in his breathing and his speech; then, in a high nasal voice, he apologized to his guests for suffering from a stomach indisposition and stumbled out of the room. As quickly as the other two could finish their dessert, coffee, and brandy, and avail themselves of the fingerbowls, they hurried into the drawing-room to offer succor; but Sir Francis was sprawled on the rug in a comatose state and died before medical assistance could be summoned.

" 'Mrs. Gabriel Gibbon was extremely distraught, and exclaimed, "I didn't think my brother-in-law looked well for some time, and I often warned him that bolting down hot-dogs was bad for his heart condition, so I really cannot claim to be surprised by this sudden cardiac seizure, although I am, of course, quite heart-broken."

" 'Her physician was called and offered her a sedative, but Mrs. Gibbon bravely insisted upon completing her duties as hostess, even demonstrating sufficient control to supervise the maids in the clearing and thorough washing and drying of the dishes, as well as the incineration of all the left-overs.

" 'Students of Debrett will recall that the Gibbon family seat, Caudal Hall, was entailed for a period of ten generations by King George III, at the time the land, titles, and rights were bestowed on the first Gibbon to be knighted. The entailing of an estate, as we are sure our readers know, means that during this period the property must be passed on and cannot be sold or otherwise disposed of. With the death of Sir Francis, this condition has now ceased to be in effect, and Mr. Gabriel is now free to dispose of the estate as he chooses, or pass it on to his heirs in legal manner. Under the conditions of the original knighthood conferred on the first Gibbon, the title also continued for this period of ten generations, so Mr. Gabriel will only be entitled to be called Sir by his servants and those friends who dislike informality.' "

Homes paused a moment to remove a boot that blocked our vision of the balance of the article, and then leaned over further, staring in utter amazement at the portion of the column that had been revealed. In a startled tone of voice, he continued:

" 'STOP PRESS: The police officials have just announced an arrest in the Caudal Hall affair, claiming that Sir Francis was the victim of none other than his guest, Mr. Wain, age 26, the American colonial. They point out that a chemist would have the necessary knowledge to administer a fatal potion in Sir Francis' food, and that despite the knight's known heart condition as testified to by his sister-in-law, they believe there is more to the matter than meets the eye, and that the heart condition was at most only a contributory factor.

" 'They note that Mr. Wain is left-handed and sat on Sir Francis' right, permitting his operative hand to constantly hover over his Lordship's food. They believe he took advantage of the fortuitous circumstance of a bitter-almond tart being served to pour oil of nutmeg, a highly toxic abortifacient, either onto the tart itself, or more likely onto the "hot-dog" itself, in a dosage sufficient to cause Sir Francis his severe abdominal pain, and eventually his death. The police base their conclusion on the faint odor of nutmeg they discerned upon the lips of the deceased, although they admit it was difficult to detect because of the almost overpowering odor of the bitter-almond tart.

" 'Whether Mr. Wain intended the dose to be fatal, the police say, is unimportant; he is nonetheless guilty of his victim's demise and shall pay the full penalty for his crime. They claim to have evidence that Mr. Wain is a revolutionary, propounding the theory that the American colonies are now independent, a viewpoint certain to have aroused the righteous wrath of so fine a patriot as Sir Francis Gibbon. Bad feelings could only have resulted, and it is the theory of the police that the dinner party developed into an argument which culminated in the tragic death of Sir Francis. Mrs. Gibbon's failure to remember any such quarrel is attributed to absent-mindedness, added to her concern over the success of the meal, which undoubtedly caused her to be inattentive. (Artist's sketches on Page 3).'

"Fools!" Homes exclaimed in disgust, replacing the boot and rewrapping the package. "Balustrade is an idiot!" He flung himself into a chair, looking up at me broodingly. "We must help this poor fellow Wat, Wainey—I mean, Wain, Watney!"

"But, Womes—I mean Homes," I said remonstratingly, "it appears to me that they have a strong case against the young man. As a medical practitioner I admit that stomach pain is often found to be related to heart seizure, but still, one cannot rule out the possibility of other agencies."

"Nonsense!" said Homes half-angrily. "I can understand a young man's reason for harming a complete stranger, and I can even understand a chemist carrying about a vial of oil of nutmeg on the offhand chance he might meet someone to whom he wished to give stomach indisposition. But what I cannot lead myself to believe is that a University graduate would be so ill-informed as to honestly believe the American colonies are independent!" He shook his head. "No, no, Watney, it is here that the police case falls down!"

He tented his fingers, staring fiercely and unseeingly over them through half-lidded eyes, his long legs sprawled before him. Minutes passed while I quietly sat down, remaining silent, respecting his concentration; then, of a sudden, our reveries were interrupted by the sound of footsteps running lightly up the stairs, and a moment later the door burst open to reveal a lovely young girl in her mid-twenties. She might have been truly beautiful had it not been for the tears in her eyes and the tortured expression on her face. Scarcely pausing for breath, she hurried across the room and knelt at Homes's side, grasping his two hands in hers.

"Oh, Mr. Homes," she cried beseechingly, "only you can save John Wain! In the first place, the scandal would be ruinous were a house-guest of mine to be found guilty of a crime; and besides, it would play havoc with the entire scheme!"

"You are Mrs. Gabriel Gibbon?"

"Yes. I will pay—" She paused, thunderstruck. "But how could you have possibly known my identity?"

Homes waved the question aside with his accustomed modesty, preferring to return to the problem at hand. "Pray be seated," said he, and waited until she was ensconced across from him. "I have read the account in the journal and I am also convinced that the police have made a grave error. Tell me," he continued, quite as if he were not changing the subject, "would I be correct in assuming that the cook at Caudal Manor is a fairly youngish woman? And unmarried, I should judge?"

"Indeed she is, but how you knew this I cannot imagine!"

"And did she recently have a quarrel with her fiancé?"

The young lady could only nod her head in stunned fashion.

"And one final question," Homes went on, eyeing

her steadily. "By any chance did Mr. Wain complain at table because his ale was not iced, as he was accustomed to drinking it?"

"He did, but—" The girl stopped speaking, coming to her feet and staring down at Homes almost in fear. "Mr. Homes, your ability is more than uncanny—it borders on the supernatural!" Her eyes were wide. "How could you possibly have known—?"

"There is nothing mystical in it," Homes assured her gravely. "In any event, you may return home with an untroubled mind. I assure you that Mr. Wain will join you—a free man—before many hours."

"I cannot thank you enough, Mr. Homes! Everything I have heard and read about you is the truth!" Her lovely eyes welled with tears of gratitude as she left the room.

"Really, Homes," I said shortly, "I fail to understand any of this. What is this business of the unmarried cook and the warm ale?"

"Later, Watney!" Homes said, and picked up his greatcoat and deerstalker. "At the moment I must go out and verify a few facts, and then see to it that poor Mr. Wain is freed. These colonials suffer sufficiently from a feeling of inferiority; incarceration can only serve to aggravate it."

It was well past midnight before I heard Homes's key in the door below, but I had remained awake, a warmed kippered toddy prepared against my friend's return, my curiosity also waiting to be assuaged. He clumped up the stairs wearily, doffed his coat and hat, and fell into a chair, accepting the toddy with a nod. Then, after quaffing a goodly portion, he put the glass aside, leaned forward, and burst into loud laughter.

"It would have done you good, Watney, to see Balustrade's stare when he was forced to unlock Wain's cell and usher the young man to the street," he said with a grin. "I swear for a moment there I thought the Inspector was going to physically engage me in fisticuffs!" He chuckled at the memory and finished his kippered toddy, visibly relaxing. "And thank you, by the way, for your thoughtfulness in preparing this toddy for me. It was delicious."

"You can demonstrate your gratitude in far better manner," I said possibly a trifle tartly, for it was well past my usual bedtime, "by explaining this entire complex, incomprehensible case to me, for none of it makes the slightest sense!"

"No?" he asked incredulously. "I am rather surprised. I should have thought the medical evidence would have pointed you in the right direction. However," he continued, seeing the look on my face and, as ever, properly interpreting it, "let us begin at the beginning." He lit a Pakistani.

"First, as you well know, Watney, I respect you quite highly as a medical man, but I have also made a study in depth of toxicology. You may recall my monograph on the Buster Ketones and the Hal-loids which had such a profound effect on early Hollywood comedies—but I digress. To me the evidence presented by the article in the morning journal was quite conclusive."

His fine eyes studied my face, as if testing me. "Tell me, Watney, what precise toxicity results in the symptoms so accurately described by the writer in the journal?" He listed them on his fingers as he continued, "One: stomach disorder. Two: dimness of vision—for

100

you will remember that Sir Francis stumbled as he left the room, and yet, after living in Caudal Manor for all his sixty-two years, one must assume he could normally have made his way about blindfolded. Three: difficulty in speaking and breathing. And four: a nasal quality to his voice."

Homes looked at me inquiringly. "Well?"

"Botulism!" I said instantly, now wide-awake.

"Exactly! True, the symptoms are similar for hydrocyanic poisoning, but with the knight consuming the frankfurter, botulism was clearly indicated. My questions to young Mrs. Gibbon regarding the ale and the cook merely confirmed it."

"I beg your pardon, Homes?" I asked, completely lost once again.

"Let us take the ale first," said he, his kindly glance forgiving my obtuseness. "Certainly Mrs. Gabriel Gibbon, herself a colonial, would be aware that icing of ale is almost compulsory in the colonies, and would therefore be expected by her compatriot. The failure to do so on the part of a dedicated hostess, therefore, could only have been caused by one thing—"

"The absent-mindedness which the reporter mentioned?" I asked, eager to be of help.

"No, Watney! *The lack of ice!* Now, in a household the size of Caudal Manor, who has the responsibility for seeing that the supply of ice is adequate? Naturally, the cook. But an elderly cook with years of experience would never forget a matter as important as ice, particularly with a foreign guest expected. Therefore, the conclusion is inevitable that the cook was not elderly, but rather, on the contrary, young. Still, even young cooks who manage to secure employment in an establishment as noted as Caudal Manor are not chosen unless they are well-qualified; therefore some problem must have been preying on the young cook's mind to make her forget the ice. Now, Watney, what problem could bother a young lady to this extent? Only one concerning a male friend; hence my conclusion that she had had a quarrel with her fiancé." He spread his hands.

"But, Homes," I asked, bewildered, "what made you think of ice in the first place? Or rather, the lack of it? Merely the floe of ideas?"

"The botulism, of course, Watney! Lack of proper refrigeration is one of the greatest causes for the rapid growth of the fatal bacteria, and both Mrs. Gibbon and her friend Mr. Wain may count themselves fortunate that the organism attacked only the one frankfurter, or they might well have both joined Sir Francis in death!"

For several moments I could only gaze at my friend Mr. Schlock Homes with the greatest admiration for his brilliant analysis and masterful deductions.

"Homes!" I cried. "You have done it again! Had it not been for your brilliant analysis and masterful deductions, an innocent colonial might have gone to the gallows for a crime due, in its entirety, to a hot-dog in the knight!" Then I paused as another thought struck me. "But one thing, Homes," I added, puzzled. "What of the oil of nutmeg that the police made such a matter of?"

Homes chuckled. "Oh, that? That was the easiest part of the entire problem, Watney. I stopped at the mortuary while I was out to-night and had a look at Sit Francis' cadaver. As I had anticipated, he had taken up a new after-shave lotion with a nutmeg bouquet, and as soon as I can determine its name, I believe I shall purchase it as well."

Due to the late hour when we finally retired that night, it was well past noon when I arose and made my way to the breakfast table. Homes had not arrived as yet, but I had no more than seated myself and reached for my first spoonful of chutneyed curry when he came into the room.

He greeted me genially and seated himself, drawing his napkin into his lap. In deference to his habits I put aside my spoon for the moment and picked up the morning journal, preparing to leaf through it in search of some tidbit of news that might serve Homes as a means to ward off ennui. But I did not need to turn the page. There, staring at me from scare headlines, was an announcement that made me catch my breath.

"Homes!" I cried, shocked to the core. "A terrible thing has happened!"

He paused in the act of buttering a kipper. "Oh?"

"Yes," I said sadly. "Tragedy seems to have struck poor Mrs. Gibbon again!"

He eyed me sharply, his fishknife poised. "You mean—?"

"Yes," I said unhappily, reading further into the article. "It seems that early this morning, while taking his constitutional along Edgeware Road, Gabriel Gibbon was struck and killed by a car recklessly driving on the wrong side of the road. The police surmise the culprit may have been from the Continent, where drivers are known to use the wrong side of the road; but this is mere theory and unsupported by fact, particularly since the driver escaped and the description of the few witnesses is considered useless."

"That poor girl!" said Homes, and sighed deeply.

"Yes," I agreed. "True, she will now inherit the Gibbon fortune, but this can scarcely compensate her for the loss of her loved one!"

"True," Homes said thoughtfully. Then a possible solution came to him and he nodded. "We can only hope that her friend Mr. Wain will stand by her in her hour of need, even as she stood by him in his! In fact, I believe he is enough in my debt for me to suggest it. A telegram form, if you please, Watney—"

The Adventure
of the Briary School

I had thought these memoirs to be ended for all time, for although my notebooks contained many as-yet-untold adventures which I had been fortunate enough to share with my good friend Mr. Schlock Homes, the fact was that after Homes's retirement to the Upson Downs for the purpose of bee-farming, he forbade me to release any further details of his many cases so long as he was no longer in the profession. It would bring him too much publicity, he feared, and would not permit him the seclusion he desired so fervently.

I was therefore quite surprised, one fine summer morning in the year '72, to hear a ring at the door and moments later to have my page usher in none other than Mr. Schlock Homes himself! I had retained our old rooms at 221B Bagel Street, and at first I thought Homes had merely dropped in for a brief nostalgic visit while in town; but before I could even offer him a cold curry from the sideboard, he had called loudly down below and two large navvies came lumbering up the steps bearing his two trunks, his portmanteau, and a welter of boxes.

"Homes!" I cried in delight, coming to my feet, curry in hand. "You have come out of retirement!"

He put off answering until his gear had been placed down to his satisfaction, and then paying off the men, he closed the door behind them and fell into a chair.

"Would you mind, Watney," he inquired, "sharing your solitude after all these years?"

"Homes!" I exclaimed. "You must know better than that! It is a pleasure. But what happened to the bee-farming?"

He shook his head, a slightly puzzled frown upon his lean features.

"This bee-farming," said he, pinching his lip, "is far more difficult than one might imagine. Year after year I planted the little devils at exactly the proper depth according to my calculations, inserted what I still feel was the correct amount of fertilizer, tamped each little hill down securely, and watered them daily. Yet not one single crop did I get!"

"Possibly you used old bees?" I asked helpfully.

"No," said he, shaking his head, "nor could it have been the soil. My carrots were more than satisfactory, and my neighbor—with whom I have a slight altercation regarding boundaries—was decent enough to say that my cucumbers, which he claims are growing on his property, will end up giving me a fine pickle. Or something on that order." He sighed heavily. "No, Watney; I fear I was meant to be a private investigator and nothing more. It is a pity there is no case awaiting me. I may have merely exchanged the frustration of bee-farming for the ennui of the city."

"I doubt that, Homes," I said with a smile. "Only this morning a telegram arrived addressed to you. I was about to send the page around to return it to sender, as I have the many others, when you arrived. Here it is now."

He accepted the form from me with eager fingers, tore open the envelope, and perused its contents with his old concentration. I sat back, pleased to be once more back in harness with Homes, and watched his nostrils dilate in that fashion I recognized from the old days as indicating his allergy to cold curry.

"Ah," said he at last, a faint smile upon his face, "nothing of great merit, but still a welcome start after my years of inaction. It appears that a certain Mr. Silas Cornbuckle—a name, you note, of uncertain national origin—has asked for an appointment at ten, and"— he glanced at the mantel clock just as the bell rang—"I shall be greatly surprised if this is not our Mr. Cornbuckle now!"

He leaned back comfortably as our page ushered in a stout young man of florid complexion, dressed in an atrociously striped garment, wearing a flaxen drooping moustache, and sporting a large chain across his weskit from which dangled a huge curved ornament. Homes nodded politely, but even before he could properly greet his visitor, I interrupted, a bit smugly, perhaps.

"Come, Homes," said I, smiling. "Let us see if your years of bee-farming have or have not dulled your talents. At one time you used to brag of your ability to discern a person's nationality or occupation from his mere appearance. What say you of this gentleman?"

Homes's eyes twinkled as he readily accepted the challenge. Our guest stood frowning in puzzlement at our exchange as Homes considered the figure before him critically.

"You will note, Watney," he said at last, almost as if the years had not passed, or as if our guest were not in the room, "the clothing of our visitor is colored in red and white stripes. Since only a patriot would wear such a garment, we can only conclude our guest is from Canada. A further proof of his nationality, if further proof were needed, is the ornament on his watch-chain, which I recognize as being an elk's tooth, since elk are native to Canada.

"As for his occupation, we must consider the fact that the elk is known for its ferocity when facing dentistry of any sort, so anyone removing a tooth must be someone familiar with the ways of the beast. When we add to this the sagging shoulders, the typical stance of one trained to follow a spoor, we can state with confidence that our guest is a professional—and obviously intrepid—hunter!"

The large man stared at Homes in amazement.

"I cannot fathom how you do it, Mr. Homes!" he exclaimed, his jaw agape. "You are absolutely right in stating that I am a patriot, and I truly meant to wear my blue weskit, but I seem to have misplaced it. Actually, I am from the Colony of New Jersey, although I have often visited Canada. I am also pleased that you recognize the courage of a member of the B.P.O.E. On the name, though, you were truly remarkable. Professional Hunter is my brother-in-law; I married his sister, Intrepid. As for the sagging shoulders, they come from carrying the luggage of ten young whippersnappers, and it is in connection with them that I find myself here."

Homes nodded genially and waved a hand.

"Have the basket chair, pray," he said, "and tell me your story. I shall be happy to assist you in any manner within my power."

Our guest sank gratefully into the indicated chair and reached into his pocket, withdrawing a bit of paper. He contemplated it in frowning silence for a moment or two and then looked up, speaking earnestly.

"Mr. Homes, I am the professor of spelling at the exclusive Briary School in Woodbine, New Jersey. Each year the staff draws straws, and the loser must accompany a group of students on the Grand Tour. This year I was the unfortunate one. I will not bore you with tales of my experiences to date, but will get directly to the point.

"This morning, Mr. Homes, I found the boys passing this note among them. Since in the past I have known to my sorrow that their boisterous spirits can become excessive at times, and since I could make neither head nor tail of the contents of the note, I hastened to make inquiries as to the best advice possible, and am now here."

He reached out and presented the paper to Homes. My friend took it and studied it intently as I came to stand behind him, reading it over his shoulder. As Mr. Cornbuckle had so truthfully stated, it seemed to be pure gibberish. It was scrawled in a childish copperplate and read as follows:

"LSD party Savoy room 715. There will be lots of grass around as well, but NO heroin! We'll ship Papa Bear to the flicks."

There was no signature to this odd bit of nonsense. Mr. Silas Cornbuckle looked at Homes anxiously.

"I do pray, Mr. Homes," said he, "that you will be able to decipher this note and prove it merely to be the basis for some boyish prank and not, as I fear, something more serious."

Homes frowned at the small bit of paper in a manner which I knew indicated he had seen something in the weird phrases which had escaped both Mr. Cornbuckle and myself. When at last he raised his head his face was expressionless, but there was a fierce light hidden in his eye.

"I would hesitate to make judgement at first reading," said he, "but I fear you were quite right in seeking help in this matter. I seriously doubt if one might call this a boyish prank! May I ask a few questions?"

"Of course!"

"These boys—they were not chosen for this trip on the basis of scholastic merit, I gather?"

"I do not know how you do it, Mr. Homes!" Silas Cornbuckle exclaimed. "But the fact is they are far from our best students. However, since their parents were the only ones who could afford the voyage, they were chosen."

"Still," Homes said, his voice deceptively soft, "even though they are not particularly studious, and even though they tend towards pranks, at times they do show gentlemanly traits, do they not?"

"It is true."

"And to finish my questioning, the next stop on your Grand Tour, I imagine, would be France?"

"Amazing!" Cornbuckle murmured, his eyes wide. "But, yes. It is. We leave with the morning tide."

Homes paid no attention to the adulation in the man's eyes but nodded at him a bit abruptly.

"I suggest you remain in your quarters all day, for I hope to have an answer for you before the day is out. If you will leave your address with our page, I shall devote my entire efforts to a rapid solution of the problem!"

Once our visitor had left, Homes sprang to his feet, striding up and down the room in his old manner, his hands clasped behind his back, the note waving there from his long fingers. At last he fell into a chair, staring at the words fiercely, wriggling about in his chair in a manner I knew meant Mrs. Essex had put too much starch in his underwear.

"Homes," I asked, "can it be a code?"

"No, no!" said he, shaking his head impatiently. "It is far more intricate than that! It is quite obvious that the plan to kidnap the Chancellor is well advanced. The only problem is how to foil the dastardly plot!"

"Homes!" I exclaimed reproachfully. "Surely after all these years of absence you have not returned merely to pull my leg!"

He considered me for several moments coldly, and then answered my question with one of his own, an irritating habit he knew infuriated me.

"Have you nothing to do, Watney? Visit Albert Hall, or the British Museum? Enjoy the pleasant scenery of Putney? Or even see a patient?"

The years had not lessened my ability to read meaning into the slightest nuance in my friend's tone. I came instantly to my feet.

"As a matter of fact," I said coolly, "I have a cepillectomy scheduled, and should have been there before now."

But Homes had already forgotten my presence, and

as I left the room he was reaching for a Vulgarian and a vespa, the paper still clutched fiercely in his fingers.

When I returned some two hours later, brushing hair from my lapel, it was to find the room full of smoke and Homes smiling quite genially at me from his chair. I recognized that he had discovered the solution to the problem.

"You must forgive me, Watney," he said, waving languidly towards the sideboard and the libation he had prepared there. "But by now you should be familiar with my humors, and time was of the essence. After all, the ides of July are almost upon us, and it would not do to allow this crime to be perpetrated without raising a finger!"

I poured myself a drink and turned to face him.

"Come, Homes," I said. "You cannot possibly mean you read some intelligent meaning into those few confused scrawls! After all, I saw the note as well as you, and I swear there was nothing there that lent itself to understanding!"

Homes shook his head in disappointment.

"Really, Watney! There was everything there. The meaning was quite clear. These young lads fully intend to kidnap one of Britain's leading statesmen and hold him, obviously for ransom, in the countryside of France, confident in their ignorance that they can fool the French police. The fact that they planned this wicked deed without involving young ladies is, of course, to their credit, but it still does not mitigate the seriousness of their intent."

I stared at Homes. He read the meaning in my frown and smiled.

112

"No, Watney," said he with a chuckle. "I am not mad, nor am I pulling your leg." His face straightened into seriousness as he reached over, taking up the note. "I have sent our page for Mr. Silas Cornbuckle, and until he arrives there should be ample time to explain this business to you."

He leaned over, placing the note on a table where we both might peruse it at the same time.

"It was really quite simple, Watney," he began. "Let us consider this note. It reads: *'LSD party Savoy room 715. There will be lots of grass around as well, but NO heroin! We'll ship Papa Bear to the flicks.'* As I had previously deduced from reading this, the boy writing these words was obviously a poor student. While I was too polite to mention the fact to Mr. Cornbuckle, since he is their professor, the spelling is atrocious."

His thin finger came out, pointing.

"For example, take the word 'Savvy,' a common colonial slang expression. And the word 'room' used as the abbreviation of the word Roman. Or 'flicks,' which is never spelled with a 'k.' Not to mention omitting the final 'e' from the word 'heroin.' " He shook his head. "Shocking!"

"But, Homes," I exclaimed a bit plaintively, "I still do not understand!"

Homes shook his head sadly at my ignorance.

"Really, Watney!" he said, and sighed. "Ah, well, let us start at the beginning, then. 'LSD' is obviously 'Pounds, Shillings, Pence.' Therefore the 'LSD party' can be nobody but the Chancellor of the Exchequer. The 'room 715'—or, more properly spelled, 'Rom. 715'—refers to the Roman calendar for the seventh month, the fifteenth day, or—as you may know—to-morrow's date. This afternoon I verified, as I had suspected, that the Chancellor travels to-night by the channel steamer for a conference in Paris."

"But what made you suspect France in the first place?" I asked, amazed as always at the constant proof of Homes's brilliance.

"Note the last line, Watney." Homes pointed to the paper. " 'We'll ship Papa Bear to the flicks.' In the colonies they have a mascot known as Smokey; it can only be he to whom 'Papa Bear' can refer. When we consider that the French police are know as 'flics,' the entire message becomes clear."

He leaned back, considering me gravely. "On the basis of our analysis, let us now re-read the note. It says: The Chancellor of the Exchequer, understand? To-morrow July 15th. (We'll hide him) in the country-side—the reference to grass, of course. No girls will be allowed to participate. We'll put down a smoke-screen for the French police."

I brought my dazed eyes up from the slip of paper.

"Marvellous, Homes," I breathed worshipfully. Then I saw a problem. "But, Homes!" I cried. "At this late hour, how can this foul scheme be scotched?"

"Easily—" he began, and then paused as the sound of footsteps on our stairs could be heard. A moment later Mr. Silas Cornbuckle burst into our quarters.

"Mr. Homes!" he cried. "I pray you have the answer! What did the message intend to convey?"

"I cannot reveal that," Homes replied quietly. "It could do nothing but damage the already tenuous ties between the American colony and the mother country. However, I can tell you how to avoid any unpleasant consequences from your charges' intended deed."

"Of course, Mr. Homes," said Silas Cornbuckle. "What can I do?"

"You must cancel France from your tour," Homes said. "There is no other solution."

Mr. Silas Cornbuckle stared at my friend. "But the boys—"

"—will doubtless be disappointed," Homes said, concluding the other's sentence. "I am sure," he added dryly, and shrugged. "Well, one cannot have everything. However, if you wish a suggestion, you might consider giving the lads a special treat as compensation."

Mr. Cornbuckle grasped the recommendation eagerly. "Such as?"

"Well," Homes said, considering the matter, "I imagine an evening at one of our local hostelries might help them get over their disappointment. In fact," he added, "it might even be better if you left them to their own devices, thus indicating your faith in their ability to entertain themselves properly." He smiled at our guest genially. "To while away the hours while the lads are occupied, you might go to the cinema. I have never seen the Nickelodeon, but I understand it interests many."

"It shall be as you say," Mr. Cornbuckle said, and turned to the door. He paused and bowed. "Nor can I thank you enough, Mr. Homes."

"A pleasure," Homes said, and returned the bow, as we watched Homes's first client stumble through the doorway, overcome with gratitude.

The following morning I came into the dining-room to find Homes already before me, replacing the remnants of curry with stuffed chutneys, his own favorite. As he served himself and took his place at the table,

115

I seated myself and opened the morning journal. Homes drew his napkin into his lap, speared his first chutney, and looked at me questioningly.

"Do you find anything in the paper to interest an up-coming, ambitious, and newly-investitured private investigator this morning?" he inquired in a tone that was only half-joking.

"I am not sure, Homes," I said slowly, reading further into the article which had caught my attention. "There is this, if you might be interested. It seems there was a narcotics raid at a local hotel last night, but it appears the miscreants all managed to escape. The police are seeking whatever help they can obtain."

Homes sat erect.

"As you know, Watney," said he, "at one time I myself was the victim of the foul habit. There is no traffic I consider more reprehensible! A telegram to the authorities, offering my services, if you would!" He leaned back. "Although," he added thoughtfully, "once the criminals hear that Schlock Homes is on the case, I should be gravely dubious if they do not flee the country by the first packet."

The Adventure
of the Hansom Ransom

In considering the many adventures I have been fortunate enough to share with my good friend Mr. Schlock Homes, I am forced to the amazing conclusion that his activities following his return from retirement on the Upson Downs put any of his previous efforts to shame. The man seemed determined to make up for the years lost in bee-farming; his energies were prodigious. Nor had he lost any of his remarkable abilities; if anything, the results of his analyses and deductions were more startling than ever.

For example, in going over my notes for the balance of the year '72, I find reference to cases which not only furthered the incredible legend of Homes, but which also did much to strengthen the ties between our beloved Britain and many of our former colonies. In Tel Aviv, to mention one instance, Homes was able to capture the culprit who fed doped oats to the favorite in the tough Kosher Stakes, a horse noted for its ability on heavy and wet tracks. Readers of these memoirs may recall the affair as *The Adventure of the Jewish Mudder and Fodder.*

But not all of Homes's work took him abroad; in August of that year he was of singular service to the noted author, Mr. Stanley Yelling, who was plagiarized in his famous biography, *The Tome of the Unknown Soldier.* Still more interesting to me, however, was a case which Homes resolved while his mind was on other problems, an affair I find delineated in my journal as *The Adventure of the Hansom Ransom.*

I had finished my rounds that warm September afternoon and had returned to our quarters at No. 221B Bagel Street to find Homes hunched over his study table, the room full of smoke from the pipe upon which he was puffing furiously, and the floor littered with crumpled scraps of paper from his many calculations. As I entered the room, he turned to me a face pale with bafflement.

"Homes!" I cried, frightened at his wan complexion. I instantly put my bag aside and hurried to the sideboard, pouring a generous tot of brandy. "What is the matter?"

He flourished a sheet of note-paper in my face as I hastily swallowed my drink.

"As ingenious a code as ever I have faced!" said he, grimacing. "It was delivered several hours ago, but as yet I have been unable to decipher it."

I came to stand beside him and read the telegram over his shoulder. As Homes had so accurately stated, it was obviously in code and presented itself as unintelligible jargon. It read as follows:

"Gotter see yer raht away. Hi'll stop rahnd yer flat fourish, abaht. 'Arry 'Iggins."

"Note the beastly cleverness of the writer," Homes said half-angrily, "intermixing real words with this other nonsense! The word 'see' and the word 'away,' the word 'stop' and the word 'flat.' I've tried 'see away stop flat,' 'see stop flat away,' 'away see flat stop,' 'flat stop see away.' " He paused as our doorbell suddenly rang. "But I'm afraid this puzzle must wait, for unless I am mistaken, we are about to have a visitor."

He hastily straightened his study table as our page boy ushered in a person who was pitiful in appearance. He cringed as he came to a shuffling stop before us, his head bent, his eyes cast down to his cracked shoes, his fingers nervously twisting a worn cap. He stood first on one foot and then on the other as if afraid to raise his head, until Homes took pity on the poor fellow.

"Here," he said in a kindly tone, "take that basket chair, and tell us your story. Other than the fact that by profession you are a hostler, I know nothing of your problem."

The man's face gaped in astonishment as he sank into the chair. Even I, familiar as I am with Homes's unusual powers, could not see the slightest basis for his deduction. Homes smiled at our confusion.

"It is really quite simple, Watney," said he, tenting his fingers. "The straight flat crease across the front of the trousers clearly indicates many hours of constant leaning over the edge of something approximately thirty inches from the floor. Since this is the height of a standard feeding bin, we can assume our visitor has something to do with stables. The chalk dust in the crease between the left thumb and forefinger looks suspiciously like Gentian Green, used as a germicide for cleansing saddles. Now, add to this the fact that even as our guest sits there, he unconsciously crooks the fingers of his left hand into the best position for holding reins, and there can be no doubt that for years he served as a hostler."

Our visitor gaped, his admiration for Homes's analysis visible on his face. Had he known Schlock Homes as long and as well as I have, he would not have been

119

so surprised. " 'Ow yer does it I can't imagine, Guv'-nor," he said, shaking his head, "but yer dead raht. Me name is 'Arry 'Iggins and I've been an 'ustler all me life, mostly down at the Spider and Fly Billiards Parlour. I been so upset by the loss of me boss's 'an-som I guess I forgot to wash me 'ands."

He hastily wiped the offending chalk from his fin-gers and sat more erect.

"What 'appened," said he, now visibly more at ease, "is some bloke I never seen afore in me life comes over to where I'm waitin' in front of me boss's 'ouse, see, an' me sittin' up atop the 'ansom like always, and tells me there's a sucker over at the Spider and Fly wiv more brass than skill, lookin' for a game. Well, I couldn't pass that up, could I? Course not, 'specially when the boss don't usually come down till eleven, so I asks the chap would 'e be so kind as to look arter me 'orse and buggy till I gets back, and off I goes to the Spider and Fly, but when I gets there, there ain't no more mark than straight cues! So I 'urries back to me 'ansom an' me rig is gorn!"

He shook his head lugubriously.

"Can't trust a blinkin' soul these days," he said sadly. "Went rahnd t' the coppers and they wasn't no more 'elp than a bustid leg! And I'm scared t' tell me boss. 'E wasn't too 'appy wiv me before, and this ain't goin' t' make 'im love me no 'arder!"

Homes nodded sympathetically.

"Well," he said, smiling to make our guest comfort-able, "consider me at your service. Tell me, was there anything special about this particular hansom that made it more worthy of stealing than any other?

Plastic harness-breeching-straps, perhaps? Imported check-reins? Gold-embossed hub-caps?"

"Naw!" said our guest disdainfully. "Can't imagine anyone floggin' that 'ansom wiv so many new ones practically askin' to be stole. This was mostly used for shoppin', this 'ansom was, only the big four-in-'and is in the shop wiv a sprung yoke, so me boss asks me to drive 'im abaht in this one. Matter of fact, I figures at first the chap just got tired of waitin' and went orf and me 'orse followed 'im, me 'orse bein' a friendly-type beast."

"A possibility," Homes conceded. "And may I ask who your employer might be?"

"Well," said the little man, " 'e might be the Queen o' the May, but 'e ain't. I 'eard that one on the telly," he added in hasty apology. "Actually, 'e's some big-wheel foreigner from be'ind the Iron Curtain. 'Eads up their Embassy 'ere in Lunnon. But we ain't supposed to mention no names."

"I see." Homes nodded. "And the man you left in charge of your hansom?"

"Never seen the bloke before," said our guest, "but 'e was a big one, 'e was! Seven foot tall at least, twenty stone of weight if an ounce, wiv a bad limp in one leg an' a big brush of orange 'air."

Homes shot erect in his chair, his nostrils flaring.

" 'Omes!" I cried. "I mean, Homes! What is it?"

"Later!" he said fiercely, and turned his attention back to our visitor. "Is there any other information you can furnish which might be of help?"

"That's abaht the lot, Guv'nor," the little man said, sad to be of such little use in his own behalf. He sounded wistful. "I don't suppose yer would consider takin' on a little no-account case like this, would yer, sir?"

"I would not miss it for the world!" Homes replied fervently, and came to his feet. "Well, since I imagine you can be reached at this Spider and Fly Billiards Parlour at any time, it is needless for you to leave an address. Be assured I shall get right to it and advise you of the outcome of my investigation as soon as possible."

He waved aside the small man's profuse attempts to thank him, and was already pacing the floor, his brow furrowed in thought and his hands locked behind his back, even before our page had shown our guest to the street.

"Really, Homes," I said in mild surprise. "I have seldom seen you so wrought. And merely over a hansom whose horse has undoubtedly wandered away!"

"Are you deaf?" he inquired, swinging upon me suddenly. "Sometimes I fear for you, Watney! Did you not hear the description of the man with whom our small friend left his hansom? Think, Watney, think! Does it not strike a familiar chord?"

I considered the little man's description carefully: seven feet tall, twenty stone of weight, a bad limp in one leg, and a shock of orange hair. I was about to deny any recognition when I saw a faint chance. "You are thinking of Professor Marty, Homes?" I asked. "The one they call—with reason—The Butcher?"

"We cannot overlook the possibility, Watney!"

"True, Homes," I conceded, thinking about it. "Certainly Professor Marty never does anything on a small scale. Should he now be involved in a scheme to steal all means of transport, within a very short time he could bring all London to its feet!"

"I doubt that is his motive," said Homes, shaking his head. "With the shortage of parking space, such an effort would be doomed to failure. Where in all London would he find room for more than two or three?" He paced the floor in thought, seeking an answer. Suddenly his head came up. "Unless—"

"Yes, Homes?" I asked eagerly.

"Our client said the hansom was an old one, did he not?"

"He did."

"I believe I have it!" Homes exclaimed and fell into a chair, beginning to scribble on pieces of paper with pen and ink.

"Homes," I said reproachfully, "with a problem involving the Professor upon us, you have gone back to the puzzle of the note delivered this morning!"

"No, no," said he, continuing to scribble. "I should like to, for it bothers me to leave it unsolved, but what I am writing is for the Professor. If you would be so kind as to have our page round up the Bagel Street Regulars, I am sure we will be in a position to scotch this nefarious scheme of the Professor's in a very short time!"

To this end I hastened to summon our page and give him proper instructions, while Homes—reminded by me, I am afraid—returned to the puzzle of the morning message, but before he could get much beyond "stop flat see away" and "stop see away flat," the Bagel Street Regulars came swarming up the stairs, under the leadership of a ragged small street arab known, in the current fashion of name and initial, as Hasser I. Homes put aside the cryptic message, a bit reluctantly, I thought, and gave them their orders.

"A tall man, at least seven feet in height," said he sternly, while they hung on every word. "He weighs about twenty stone. He limps badly and has bright orange hair. I have identical notes for each of you; the one who locates him will give it to him. I suggest you split up, each taking a different billiard parlor, since these seem to be his usual base of operations. And tuppence-ha'penny extra for the brave lad who first locates him!"

I turned to him as the lads fled eagerly down the steps, each clutching his note tightly. "Your note to the Professor?" I asked, mystified.

"Merely an invitation to him for a chat," he said enigmatically, and returned at once to the crumpled sheet of paper upon his study table. And so passed the following hour, silent except for his occasional mutter, *sotto voce,* " 'Flat see away stop'? 'Flat stop away see'? It is impossible! 'Away flat stop see'? 'See spot—I mean stop—' But here is one of our Regulars back already, I do believe."

It was Hasser I, and he catapulted into the room, panting.

"I have located him, Mr. Homes!" he said proudly, fighting for breath. "He is involved in a snooker game at a billiard parlor in Limehouse called The Quicksand Club."

"You gave him my note?" Homes demanded fiercely.

"I did, indeed, sir. He was in the middle of a long run and said he would be along as soon as he finished."

"Good," Homes said, and reached for his purse.

"Here is a shilling for each lad involved in the hunt, as well as the extra bonus I promised you. Well done, Hasser I!" Homes fell back into his chair as the lad went clattering down the steps. "Well, Watney," he continued, as the front door slammed, "I hope this affair with the Professor can soon be settled, for the matter of this infernal coded message is beginning to prey upon my mind."

"How do you plan on handling the Professor, Homes?" I asked curiously. "Quite simply," he said, but before he could continue there was a loud sound in the passage and the door to our quarters burst open. Professor Marty brusquely brushed aside our page and came to stand above Homes, glaring down.

"Homes," he said gratingly, "what is the nonsense contained in this note?" He pulled a slip of paper from his pocket, dug about in his weskit for his spectacles, and read aloud in a sneering tone. " 'Professor Marty, you will kindly forget about holding the foreign hansom for ransom and return it at once! Signed, Schlock Homes.' "

Homes nodded to him politely, but his face was expressionless and his voice cold.

"If you will take the large chair, Professor, I shall be pleased to explain." He waited until the Professor had sunk into the chair before continuing. "In the first place, there could never have been the slightest doubt as to why you stole that trap yesterday—"

"I needed something to run around in—"

Homes disregarded him. "Considering the age and lack of special features, the carriage undoubtedly falls into the category of an antique, and therefore must be quite valuable. As a valuable antique, it must therefore be worthy of a substantial ransom."

"I never thought of that," Professor Marty mumbled, shaking his head.

"However," Homes continued sternly, paying no attention to the man's mumbling, "it makes no difference as to its value. Since I am onto your scheme, there is nothing for you to do now but admit failure and return the carriage to its rightful owner."

Professor Marty started up, his face red. His voice was a growl.

"And what makes you think I'll do a fool thing like that?"

"Because, if you do not, I shall make London too hot to hold you," Homes returned, his eyes narrowed. He continued to hold the Professor in his steady gaze. "In addition to returning the hansom, you will write a note of apology to the owner. You will say you are sorry you took the hansom, and in compensation for the time you used it, you will send him some small present."

"You're mad!"

"You will send him some small present," Homes repeated firmly. "Let me see . . . To-morrow being Thursday, the traditional day for English servants to enjoy their liberty, a thoughtful gesture would be some affair to save the mistress of the house the task of cooking their evening dinner. The Bow Street Banquet, for example, or comps to McDonalds—"

"Now you just wait a minute!" Professor Marty began in a roar, and then suddenly calmed down. He leaned forward in his chair, his tiny piggish eyes intent upon Homes's stern visage. "You say return the trap. You then suggest that to-morrow night—the servants' night out—I send these people tickets which will also

126

take them from their home—to a banquet, that is, of course. Is that your suggestion?"

"It is not a suggestion," Homes said coldly. "It is a demand."

Professor Marty came to his feet with an effort.

"Homes," he said with deep feeling, "you are a find! I mean a fiend!" He shrugged hopelessly. "I have no choice. It shall be as you say." He sighed and limped from the room, a broken man.

"You have done it again, Homes!" I exclaimed in admiration, but my friend merely shrugged off the compliment and returned to his study table, glowering down at the sheet of note-paper which seemed intent upon perplexing him as no other problem had since I had known him.

I came to breakfast the following morning to find Homes dozing fitfully in his chair, the lamp still burning and the floor covered with the refuse of his calculations. Fearing for his well-being should he continue to concentrate on this one problem, I hastened to open the morning journal in search of some more interesting divertissement, just as he stirred and sat up, stretching. I considered him anxiously.

"No luck, Homes?"

"None," he said glumly. "It is fiendish! And yet I am sure the answer is in those simple four words: 'see,' 'away,' 'stop,' and 'flat.' I have even tried the first letters in all combinations; they form 'sasf,' 'fass,' 'fsas,' 'assf,' 'ssaf'—"

"Come, Homes," I said soothingly, "let me have Mrs. Essex fix you a nice plate of creamed chutneys. You know how they always calm you."

He considered me balefully. "Do not commiserate with me, Watney! Nor treat me as an invalid!"

"Never, Homes," I said as I hurriedly turned the pages of the newspaper. Suddenly I sat erect, certain I had the solution to my friend's problem.

"Homes," I exclaimed, "here is a case which I am sure will interest you. Last evening the dwelling of Stannous Fluoride, the Polish Ambassador, was burgled! It seems all the servants were out, and the Ambassador and his wife had accepted an invitation to dine at some banquet or other—"

"No, no, Watney," said he wearily. "I should enjoy resolving the problem, since I feel strongly about treatment afforded guests of our Government, but I cannot give up so easily on this puzzle."

He returned to the crumpled paper before him, and then suddenly all trace of sleepiness fled from his countenance.

"Watney!" he cried, excitement flushing his face. "I am a fool! The answer is simplicity itself!" He swung about, one finger still pointing to the sheet of paper on his study table. "My error was in discounting the writer's ability to misspell!"

"Homes," I exclaimed, "what do you mean?"

"I mean it was not the *word* 'see'—it is the *letter* 'C'! The message now becomes crystal-clear!" His thin finger pointed. *"C stop away flat.* It can only refer to the C-stop of the giant organ at Albert Hall, since it is the only organ I am familiar with! Fortunately, I am still in possession of the tuning fork I won at a bean-eating contest in my second year at public school. A note to the organist at the Hall, if you please, Watney, offering my services."

128

The Adventure of the
Great Train Robbery

It was rare, indeed, for my good friend Mr. Schlock Homes and myself to disagree as to the merits of his ability in resolving a case, yet such a situation arose in regard to an affair which I find reference to in my notebook as *The Adventure of the Great Train Robbery*. In my estimation, the case allowed Homes as great a use of his exceptional powers as any I can recall, but the fact was that Homes himself was far from satisfied with his performance in the matter. I can but leave it to the reader to judge for himself.

It was upon a Wednesday, February 31st, that we first heard of Sir Lionel Train. Homes had been exceptionally busy those early months of '68, first with the problem of the championship kittens stolen just hours prior to an international show, a case I find referred to as *The Adventure of the Purloined Litter,* following which my friend went on to resolve the curious puzzle of a punch-drunk prize-fighter, a case I later chronicled as *The Adventure of the Rapped Expression.* It was not, therefore, until the final day of February that the matter of Sir Lionel came to our attention.

This particular Wednesday the weather had turned quite poor, with a night of fierce snow followed by dismal skies and a sharp drop in temperature. Homes, therefore, had given the day over to relaxation and was bent over his laboratory bench, with me in sharp

129

attendance, studying some putty-like material called "Plastique" he had received without comment just that morning from his old friend M'sieu C. Septembre Duping in Paris. We had already noted its color and odor, as well as its rubber-like consistency, and Homes was about to strike it with a hammer to test the resilience of the strange material when there came a sudden disturbance on the stairway, and a moment later Homes's brother Criscroft had burst in upon our scientific experiments.

It was extremely odd for Criscroft to appear at our quarters at 221B Bagel Street without prior notice, and even more unusual to see that normally most controlled of gentlemen gasping for breath. His clothing was awry, his gaiters unbuckled, and there was an air of urgency about him which communicated itself at once to Homes's razor-sharp instincts. Homes immediately replaced the putty-like substance in its wrapping, returned the hammer to its proper place in the tool rack, washed and dried his hands carefully, and, wasting no time, faced his brother.

"Well, Criscroft," said he, lighting a Vulgarian, "this is indeed a pleasure! But you appear disturbed— or have I misinterpreted the signs?"

Criscroft fell into a chair, still fighting for his composure.

"As usual you are correct, Schlock!" he exclaimed. "We may well be in deep trouble, indeed! I fear some grave misfortune may have befallen Sir Lionel Train."

Homes nodded in instant understanding. "Who?" he inquired.

"Sir Lionel Train, head of Q6-JB45-VX-2DD-T3, the most secret of our secret services. Other than the

Yard and Special Services, no one has ever heard of
the man."

"Ah! *That* Sir Lionel Train!" Homes said, and nodded. "Pray favor us with the details."

"Very well," Criscroft said. He sat a bit more erect,
obviously relieved to have his brother's aid with the
dire problem. "Well, then, the facts are these! Sir Lionel has his country estate at Much-Binding-
in-the-Groyne, a typical English village near Tydin,
Notts, where he spends his mid-weeks with his famous
diamond collection. In any event, early this morning
a neighbor of his, out to check the weather, happened
to notice Sir Lionel struggling in hand-to-hand com-
bat with an assailant in his bedroom. Not wishing to
be hasty, this neighbor returned to his house and took
up a pair of binoculars, with which he verified the sight
he had seen. Satisfied he had not been incorrect—for
through the binoculars he could see this unrecogniz-
able assailant's hands around Sir Lionel's neck—he
immediately sent his butler off to Scotland Yard with
the information."

"He did not interfere directly?"

"Of course not. They had never been introduced."

"I understand. But he continued to watch?"

"He had come out without his slippers. No, once his
butler had been sent off, this neighbor repaired to his
basement, where he is building a bottle-in-a-ship."

"I see. And Scotland Yard—?"

"Aware of Sir Lionel's true status, the Yard instantly
communicated with the Home Office, who in turn sent
a messenger to advise me. When my man could not
locate a cab, I hastily dressed and ran all the way.
Schlock, you must go to Much-Binding-in-the-Groyne

immediately and do everything in your power to save Sir Lionel!''

Homes considered his brother steadily behind tented fingers.

"At what hour did this neighbor note Sir Lionel struggling?"

"A bit before seven this morning."

"It is just after noontime. It is possible, of course, that I may arrive too late. However, we can but try. Tell me, where was Lady Train during all this?"

"Lady Train is visiting relatives."

"Sir Lionel has no staff?"

"Just a new maid he employed only yesterday, right after Lady Train left. Sir Lionel has an aversion to butlers."

"I see. But regarding your fears, surely Sir Lionel does not keep state secrets in his country home?"

Criscroft shook his head decisively.

"Sir Lionel commits nothing to paper. Still, under the duress of torture, who knows what secrets he might divulge?" Criscroft came to his feet. "It is in your hands, Schlock," he said. With an abrupt nod in our direction he stepped on a gaiter buckle and stumbled heavily down the stairs.

"Ah, well, Watney," said Homes with a sigh, "a pity our afternoon is to be compromised. They are playing the Hayden Go Seek concerto at Albert Hall and I had hoped to attend. However, duty before pleasure. You might bring along your medical bag, as it seems it might be useful. And you might also bring along Duping's gift. Studying it might help us while away an hour or so on the train."

The Nottingham Express dropped us off in Tydin,

and a rented trap was easily arranged with the station-master. He also furnished us with directions to Sir Lionel's estate, and moments later we were driving smartly along the newly cleared road to Much-Binding-in-the-Groyne.

Here in Nottinghamshire the sun had wormed its way through the heavy overcast, a blanket of glistening snow stretched across the endless fields, and ice glittered on wires that hung between each house and a line of poles inexplicably planted in a row along the highway. Had our mission not been of such serious intent, we might well have enjoyed the brisk air and lovely scenery.

Sir Lionel's home lay around a curve beyond the quaint village. We passed the village green, crossed a small burn lightly crusted with ice, and slowed down as we approached the house. I was about to direct our trap down the carriage-way when Homes suddenly placed a hand upon my arm. I pulled our panting horse to a stop and looked at my friend inquiringly.

"From here on it would be best if we proceeded by foot," said he, his eyes sparkling with the excitement of the chase. "Note the unbroken expanse of snow. It would not do to disturb it without first seeing if it can answer any of our questions."

"True," I admitted, and looked about for a weight to throw down, but it seems our station-master had overlooked putting one into the carriage. Homes noted my search and shook his head.

"Block the wheels with Duping's package," said he impatiently. "Time may be of the essence."

Shamed at not having thought of the simple solution myself, I dropped from the trap, propped the wheel against the horse's wandering, and turned to Homes, medical bag in hand. But Homes's attention was already directed towards the smooth snow that stretched on all sides of the manor house. A frown appeared on my friend's lean face, to be replaced almost at once by a look of determination.

"Come!" said he, and started off on a large circuit of the grounds with me close upon his heels. The snow lay unblemished in all directions. We passed the stables at the rear of the coach-house to one side, and at last came about our huge circle to our starting point. Suddenly my companion froze in his tracks.

"Homes!" I cried in alarm, since the temperature was not that low. "What is it?"

"Later," said he fiercely, and dropped to one knee to study intently two pairs of footprints beside our trap which I swear had not been there upon our arrival. I waited in silence as my companion checked them thoroughly, and then watched as he slowly rose to his feet with a frown, brushing the snow from his trousers.

"Two men," said he slowly. "One tall and thin, and from the angle of his prints, of rather intense nature. The other is short and walks with a slight limp. I should say without a doubt that the shorter of the two is a medical man by profession, and a bit absent-minded in the bargain."

"Really, Homes!" I exclaimed reproachfully. "I can understand that you might arrive at the relative heights of the men by the lengths of their stride, but surely you are pulling my leg when you claim one of them to be a medical man—and an absent-minded one, at that!"

"At times I wonder at you, Watney," said Homes

134

impatiently. "You have forgotten that today is
Wednesday, the traditional day for doctors to leave
their practice to their nurse and take to the open air.
You have also failed to properly examine the tracks
this man left; had you done so you would have noted
that the shorter of the two is wearing golfing shoes.
Since the snow is too deep for playing the game, one
can only assume he put them on automatically before
leaving the house, an action which not only clearly
indicates his absent-mindedness, but also serves as
further proof of his profession, since on Wednesdays
doctors don them from force of habit."

"He might have been a dentist," I hazarded a bit
sullenly, although in truth I did not doubt the accuracy
of Homes's masterful analysis.

"No, Watney," said he. "Dentists, from constant
standing, develop much larger feet. But we are wasting time. The two men undoubtedly passed as we were
in the rear near the stables. However, since their spoor
does not approach the house, it is evident they have
gone off about their business and have nothing to do
with the case. Come!"

He turned and moved off towards the house, breaking trail through the snow, while I followed as quickly
as my shorter legs would permit. A moment later and
Homes was stamping the loose snow from his boots
on the porch, while examining the lock on the main
door with narrowed eyes.

"Homes!" I exclaimed as a sudden thought struck
me. "I should have also brought my revolver! Surely
if there are no footprints in the snow, the assailant
must still be within the house, for there is no other
exit."

"You forget the overhead wires leading to those

poles in the road," he said, reaching into his pocket for his set of picklocks. "They have obviously been placed on each house to afford an auxiliary means of exit from the upper stories in case of emergencies; otherwise what purpose would be served by the spikes in the poles, forming a ladder? No, Watney, our assailant would have no problem leaving the house without leaving footprints, especially if he were small."

I nodded in admiration for Homes's analysis, and then followed my friend into the silent house as the door quickly succumbed to the magic of his touch. We made our way through the main hall and up the steps of the grand stairway. At its head an open door leading to the library revealed a large safe standing ajar. Homes shook his head pityingly.

"Had the miscreant known, as we do, that Sir Lionel commits nothing to paper, he might have saved himself the trouble of struggling with that heavy safe," said he. "But let us continue our search."

We moved from the library, making our way along the balcony that fronted the floor below across an ornate railing. As we reached the corner, a sudden guttural sound brought us up short, and a moment later Homes was dashing down a hallway in the direction of the strangled noises. I followed in all haste, my medical bag banging against my thigh. Homes threw open a door and paused abruptly.

"It is Sir Lionel himself!" he said, turning to me. "Pray God we are not too late. It is in your hands now, Watney."

I hastened to the side of the bed and bent over the man. He lay on his back, one arm dangling helplessly over the side of the large mussed bed. Sir Lionel was wearing his pajama bottoms, but his chest was bare, and even as I watched, it rose and fell, accompanied by his stentorian breathing.

"Homes," I said in a low voice, "the poor man has been badly treated, indeed. Note the scratches on his shoulders; note the puckered red blotches on his cheeks and lips; smell the sweet odor, similar to Chanel Number Five, doubtless one of the new perfumed anaesthetics."

"But he put up a brave struggle from the appearance of the bedclothes," Homes commented.

"Which probably saved his life," said I, and reached down and shook the man gently. "Sir Lionel!"

"Not right now, darling," he muttered, and opened his eyes sleepily. They widened incredulously at sight of my face. "Eh, what? Who? What, what? What? Who, what, what?" He turned and saw my companion. "Schlock Homes! How much did my wife pay—"

"The poor chap is completely incoherent, Homes," said I, and plunged the needle of my hypodermic into his bare arm. "The shock of sudden rescue often does this to people."

Sir Lionel's head fell back onto the pillow. I pulled his arm up to fold it across his chest and then paused.

"Homes!" I ejaculated.

"Yes?" said he.

"Look here," I said, and pointed to a tattoo that ran across the biceps and which had been revealed as I drew up his arm. "What do you make of this?"

Homes moved swiftly to my side and read the tattoo over my shoulder.

" 'Left 36, Right 21, Left twice to 15, Right 9.' " My friend straightened up, staring at the mysterious symbols with a bitter look in his eyes. "Criscroft stated that Sir Lionel never committed secrets to paper, but he said nothing of a tattoo!"

"But surely those numbers can have but little significance, Homes," I said, hoping to soothe him. "They are probably merely the result of a boyish prank from his University days."

"I doubt it is that simple," Homes replied heavily. "They are obviously references to the political left and right. Undoubtedly the numbers delineate the code name of our secret agents in certain countries of both persuasions." He shook his head. "Come, Watney. If Sir Lionel is settled for the moment, let us continue our search of the house for more clews."

I hastily tucked a cover to Sir Lionel's chin and followed Homes as he moved from the room. Our search was more thorough this time, starting in the cellars, including the kitchens, and returning to the upper stories. At the far end of the final corridor we came upon a narrow set of steps leading to the attic rooms, and Homes took them evenly, with me upon his heels.

At the top a small landing beneath the eaves revealed a door set between dormers and partially open. Homes peered cautiously around the jamb and then stepped swiftly back, drawing me into the shadows. From my new vantage point I could see into the room; a young lady was bending over a small attaché-case, tucking a chamois bag into its depths. Homes gripped my arm painfully.

"Do you see that young lady?" he demanded in a taut whisper. "That, Watney, is none other than Miss

Irene Addled, international jewel thief, and the only woman who ever bested me! And yet, see to what sad end she has come. Despite the proceeds of years of crime, see where she has ended—a maid of all work in a small country manor house! There is a lesson here for all of us, I am sure, but unfortunately, there is no time to explore it. Come!"

He pushed his way into the small room. The young lady looked up from closing her small case and then shrank back against the wall, aghast at sight of my companion.

"Mr. Schlock Homes!" she cried in terror. "What are you doing here?"

"It is all right, Miss Addled," Homes said gallantly. "I am not here in respect to you, nor am I one to bear a grudge, especially against one upon whom evil days have so obviously fallen. Still, I fear I have some bad news for you. Your master has been viciously attacked. However, thanks to Dr. Watney, he is resting comfortably. I suggest you go down and sit by his bedside. It will comfort him to see a friendly face upon awakening."

"And then may I leave?"

"As soon as the ambulance arrives. Dr. Watney and I shall go for one at once. I realize this means the end of your new-found employment, but if you stop by our quarters I shall do my best to see if I can arrange suitable employment in some other ménage."

"Some day, somehow, I shall find some means of thanking you!" she cried, and flung her arms about his neck, still holding her attaché-case. Homes reeled back, blushing, while Miss Addled hurried down the steps. Homes and I followed and watched as the thankful young lady moved towards the master bedroom with a remarkable sense of direction considering her few hours in the house. With the matter settled, Homes and I descended the main staircase and walked out onto the porch. Suddenly Homes stopped so abruptly that I ran into him from behind.

"Homes!" I said in a muffled voice. "What is it?"

"I am a fool!" he cried.

"But why?" I insisted.

His thin finger pointed dramatically. "We have been followed!"

I came from behind him and stared. It was true! The same two sets of footprints that had so mysteriously appeared beside our trap were now facing us again, leading directly to the house. There was no mistaking the long stride of the taller man, nor the spike-marks of the shorter.

"I am an idiot!" Homes cried. "I should have realized the only reason Sir Lionel was left alive was precisely because he had *not* revealed the secret of that tattoo, despite the terrible torture. Obviously, the smaller man left the house by means of the overhead wires for the purpose of bringing an accomplice, a larger person to exert greater pressure on Sir Lionel. And, locating the accomplice, the two returned to the house."

"But where are they now, Homes?" I cried.

"Obviously, they heard our sounds of search and have gone away. But these footprints are still quite fresh, Watney! They cannot have gotten very far. Come! After them!"

With a bound from the porch we dashed through

the snow to our trap and scrambled inside, not even wasting time to unblock the wheels. I cracked the whip close beside our horse's ear, and with a convulsive leap he sprang forward. My last conscious memory as we rose in the air under the force of an explosion was of Homes's voice tinged with a bitterness I had seldom heard before.

"I am a *double* fool!" he cried. "Allowing them to booby-trap us!"

It was several weeks before we were released from St. Barts and allowed to return to the ministrations of Mrs. Essex. Sir Lionel Train, obviously unnerved by the events, had gone off to the continent on a protracted holiday with a young nurse, and we had had no word from poor Miss Addled. But despite what I consider one of Homes's most brilliant successes, he continued to consider it a failure and to brood heavily upon it.

"Look, Homes," I said at breakfast the first day we were able to be up and about, "after all, Sir Lionel suffered no permanent harm, and that was your major assignment. Nor was the secret of the code numbers ever revealed, since the explosion apparently frightened the villains away. And as for poor Miss Addled, I am sure your paths will cross again one day. So how can you possibly consider this case a failure?"

"You do not understand, Watney," said he bitterly, reaching for a curried curry. "It is the fact that we had those nefarious criminals within our grasp and allowed them to escape! And not only to escape, but to hamper our pursuit by planting an explosive practi-

141

cally under our noses. How does one live down an insult of such dimensions? How, in addition, does one advise an old friend like M'sieu C. Septembre Duping that, due to my idiocy, his gift to me was destroyed? No, Watney, I shall not rest until I lay those two rascals by the heels!"

There being no arguing with Homes when he was in this mood, I turned to the morning *Times*, hoping to discover some interesting case which might take my friend's mind from his obsession. Suddenly, a new feature, imported from the American colonies, struck my eye.

"Homes!" I cried. "I do believe you will find this of interest."

He reached over and removed the journal from my hand. I watched his eyes narrow as he noted the design I had been studying. Suddenly he struck his fist upon the table, causing the chived chives to jump.

"There can be no doubt, Watney. It is they!" said he with deep satisfaction. "Note the silk topper worn by the shorter of the two—surely the sign of Harley Street affluence. And note the rather stupid expression on the face of his taller accomplice, for had he not been stupid he would never have crossed swords with Schlock Homes. A pity we should find them by pure chance, but better this way than not at all." He reached for his magnifying-glass. "What are their names again?"

I came to read over his shoulder. "Mutt and Jeff," I replied.

"Precisely! A letter to the editor of the *Times* at once, Watney, if you will!"

The Adventure of Black, Peter

It is some years since the events I am about to speak of occurred, mainly owing to our housekeeper Mrs. Essex's use of one of my journals as a doorstop; but it is still with admiration, after all this time, that I am able to report of the uncanny ability of my good friend Mr. Schlock Homes in solving a problem that had baffled the best brains of Scotland Yard. Nor did the case come at a bad time, for Homes was at a loose end, having just resolved the singular affair of the circus performer who swallowed electric-light bulbs for a living, a case my readers may recall as *The Adventure of the Illustrious Client,* and was more than ready for a new challenge.

It was a stormy Wednesday morning in early March, with sheets of icy rain beating our window panes, and the coal-fire in our quarters at 221B Bagel Street a welcome buffer against the chill of the elements. Homes was curled up in his easy chair, violin in hand, toying with the slow movement of Copeland's Cymbal Concerto, while I was deep in research, studying a treatise on digital serum injections, *Vaccinations on a Thumb,* by Hayden, when there came a loud pounding on our street door, and a moment later our page was announcing a visitor. Homes and I exchanged curious glances, since neither of us was expecting company, but I dutifully dog-eared my page while Homes laid aside his violin and came to his feet.

To our great surprise, the man who appeared dripping in the doorway was none other than Inspector "Giant" Lestride, one of the original Bow Street runners, and certainly not one of Homes's closest admirers. Homes frowned but, in his hospitable manner, waved the man to enter.

"Come in, Inspector. Have a chair. Let me have your things."

The large man removed his bowler and macintosh and accepted a chair by the fire, while Homes, after disposing of the garments, returned to his own chair. There were several moments of silence before Lestride cleared his throat and spoke.

"I may as well be blunt from the beginning, Mr. Homes," he said. "This visit was none of my doing. But the Assistant Commissioner insisted that we consult you on a rather interesting case that has come our way." He shrugged. "I seriously doubt you can be of any aid when the best brains of the Yard have been unsuccessful, but the A.C.'s word is law."

"And precisely what is this case you refer to?" Homes inquired evenly.

Lestride withdrew his notecase, opened it to extract a folded slip of paper, and handed it across to Homes. My friend accepted it and leaned back to study it, his face expressionless. I stepped behind him to read it over his shoulder. It had been typed on a standard telegraph form and read quite simply:

BARCLAYS WEDNESDAY MIDNIGHT SOUP YOUR RESPONSIBILITY QUICKLOCK-TYPE VAULT

Homes fingered the note a moment and then looked up with a frown. "Where did you obtain this, Inspector?"

"We found it on the person of a man named Peter Black, but known to his intimates—for reasons we cannot fathom—as Peteman Black. He was picked up this morning on a routine charge of mopery with intent to gawk, and in the course of our regular search we discovered this telegram. Since our code experts could not make anything of it, we felt it highly suspicious. And, of course, unless a solution is discovered before eight o'clock this evening we shall be forced to release this man Black, since the maximum we can hold a person on his charge without additional evidence is twelve hours."

Homes nodded thoughtfully. "And this man Black, what does he do for a living?"

"Well," said Lestride, "he claims to work for Reuters, the news agency people, in some capacity that leaves him free evenings." He smiled a bit cruelly. "I can see you're stumped, Mr. Homes. Admit it."

"Since your people have had the message most of the morning, and I have just this moment been handed it, I think it only fair that you withhold your opinion until I have had time to study the matter," Homes said with a cool smile. "Still, even at first glance certain things stand out."

Lestride frowned at him.

"Barclays," Homes continued evenly, "—if that is the one referred to—is, of course, one of London's leading restaurants, but I believe they normally close at ten, so bringing soup there at midnight seems a bit strange. As for the quicklock-type vault—"

He reached behind him for a reference book, opened it and studied a page for several moments, and then closed it, his finger marking the spot, while he looked at Lestride.

"Tell me," he said, "am I correct in assuming that this man Black is not a young man, but approximately my own age?"

"Why, yes, he is, Mr. Homes," Lestride answered, obviously taken aback.

"And did he serve, as did we all, in the army during the Great War?"

Lestride's jaw dropped. "As a matter of fact, he did," he said, "although how you ever guessed it is beyond me!"

"It was not a guess, but a deduction," Homes replied coolly and came to his feet, closing the reference book and returning it to its proper place. He turned back to Lestride, who also had risen. "Well, Inspector, I suggest you return at six this evening. I should have some word for you on the matter at that time."

Lestride studied Homes with suspicion for several moments and then shrugged. "Well, you have been lucky on a few occasions," he said. "If you can solve that code by this evening, I shall only be too glad to let bygones be bygones." And picking up his mac and bowler, he quickly made his way down the stairs.

" 'I shall only be too glad to let bygones be bygones'!" Homes quoted with a wry smile. "One would think I had not set him straight a dozen times in the past. Ah, well, I suppose I shall have to do it once more, for the Commissioner's sake, and still be forced to face Lestride's officiousness in the future."

"But, Homes," I cried, "how were you able to deduce the man's age and army background from those few words?"

"Later, Watney," he said in kindly fashion. "At the moment there is much to do."

146

"And do you honestly feel you can solve a code that has stumped the experts at the Yard? I do not doubt your ability, Homes," I added, "but time is so limited."

"All the more reason not to waste it, then," he said, and started to undo the cord of his dressing-gown. "And now I must go out, much as I dislike to do so in this weather."

His final words were muffled as the door closed behind him. In mystified silence I awaited his reappearance, and when at last the door to his room opened, I fear my mouth fell open in astonishment, for Homes was dressed in the garb of a soldier. And since fully thirty years had passed since he last had occasion to wear it, it was necessarily short in the shank.

The campaign hat with the acorns fitted well enough, however, and the rolled puttees—other than being a bit faded—were not too bad. With the years his swagger stick had warped a bit but was still clearly usable. He walked to the doorway with an officer's strut that was characteristic of his great acting ability, swished his swagger stick against his leg, winced, and smiled painfully at me.

"I shall return," he said with a brave grimace that left me as puzzled as admiring, and limped down the steps.

Dusk had fallen and the cold rain continued to sweep the streets when Homes at last came back. He climbed the stairway in labored fashion, flung the door shut behind him, and fell into a chair, immediately bending to loosen the tight puttees. I noted his scowling visage with concern.

"Homes," I asked anxiously, "are you all right?"

He did not answer but instead unwrapped the puttees and shook them violently. A torrent of water descended upon our rug, followed by several cigarette stubs and various other pieces of debris. "From the bottom up, not from the top down!" he muttered to himself in exasperation, and fell back into his chair. Suddenly he seemed to recall my question.

"Why, yes, Watney," he replied with a smile. "Other than being chilled and quite hungry, I am fine. What has Mrs. Essex prepared for our evening repast?"

"Pickled curries with buttered chutneys, your favorites," I replied. "But, Homes, what of the problem? What of those unintelligible words? Were you able to make any headway?"

"Of course," he said languidly, and reached behind him for a Venusian. He lit it and drew smoke into his lungs deeply, with a twinkle in his eye. I could see he was merely drawing out the suspense in that insufferable manner of his when he has finally brought some difficult problem to a successful conclusion.

"Really, Homes!" I said with a touch of asperity. "At times you are quite impossible!"

"No, no, Watney!" he said, holding up his hand. "Impossible is what you eliminate when you wish to remain with the improbable." He sighed. "All right, then, Watney, if you cannot await Lestride's arrival, I suppose I must satisfy your curiosity. The message was clarity itself, given the proper approach, and was quite natural to be on the person of Mr. Black, since he works for a news agency. It merely states that a romantic colonial with a rather odd appellation—apparently he drinks—has been fortunate enough to win a terpsichorean contest in one of our commonwealth nations. Canada, to be precise. It was just that simple."

"Really, Homes," I said reproachfully. "You gain nothing by pulling my leg!"

"Oh, I am quite serious, beli ve me!" he replied. "But here, if I am not mistaken, is Lestride himself, and you shall hear the details as I give them to him."

The door opened to reveal the large police-officer, his bowler held tightly in his hand. He made no motion to relieve himself of his dripping macintosh but stood there like a rock, his normal superciliousness asserting itself as always.

"Well, Mr. Homes," he said with a sneer, and it was evident he was prepared to enjoy my friend's discomfiture, "I assume we shall be forced to allow Mr. Black his freedom simply because you were unable to break the code."

"Come in, Inspector," Homes said warmly. "Take off your coat and have a seat. You are quite correct in stating that you will have to free Mr. Black, not because I was unable to solve the riddle of those words, but precisely because they were so easily explained."

He smiled at the startled expression on the Inspector's face, waited until the still-suspicious police official had divested himself of his outer garments and was seated, and then withdrew the slip of paper from his pocket. He placed it on a table where we could all peruse it, and laid a thin finger upon it.

"Let us consider these words," he said calmly.

'BARCLAYS WEDNESDAY MIDNIGHT SOUP YOUR RESPONSIBIL-
ITY QUICKLOCK-TYPE VAULT.' Now, Watney, you asked me
this afternoon how I was able to deduce the man's age
and army background from these few words. Well, you
were in India at the time, I believe, and the Inspector,
here, was too young to be involved; but in the extensive training we were put through to prepare us for
the trenches of France, we were taught the quicklock-
type vault as a means of leaping over enemy barbed
wire. In fact, this type vault remained in Regs until it
was pointed out that too many of our troops were
suffering from hernias as a result of keeping the knees
so tightly compressed during take-offs, after which the
quicklock was replaced by the more sensible open-
stance-type vault that I believe is in use to this day."

I stared in unashamed admiration at my friend,
while even Inspector Lestride was forced to modify
the frowning suspicion with which he had been attend-
ing Homes's words. Homes leaned back, tenting his
fingers, and continued calmly.

"Now," said he, "knowing that this Peter—or Peteman—Black was familiar with the quicklock-type vault
indicated to me he had been in the war; hence my
deduction regarding his age and past army experience." He untented his fingers long enough to raise
one of them professorially. "However, it also indicated to me something far more important."

"And what is that, Homes?" I asked breathlessly.

He smiled at me. "Consider," he said. "Here we
have a man who works for a wire service, an employment where information is often transmitted in code
either for reasons of economy, or to prevent competi-

150

tive services from stealing information. True, to us the information may not appear to be very significant, but undoubtedly it was to a born newsman."

"But what information?" Lestride asked, his attention now fully riveted upon my friend, and his sneering manner no longer in evidence. "And what possible code?"

"As to the information," Homes replied, "as I explained to Watney before your arrival, Inspector, it merely dealt with the winning of a dancing contest. And as for the code, it was the natural one for an ex-army man to use. It was the standard military vocabulary—known, I believe, as the phonetic alphabet."

Lestride stared at him. "The *what?*"

"The phonetic alphabet," Homes repeated, and turned to me. "Did they not use it in India, Watney?"

"Of course," I said instantly and quoted from memory, "Able, Baker, Charley, Dog, Echo, Fox, and so on for A, B, C, D—"

Homes held up his hand. "Ah! I also thought so, but when I applied those letters to this message, I got no results. It then occurred to me that over the years the phonetic alphabet might well have been changed. In the proper raiment, I had no difficulty in gaining access to the local Army and Navy Store, and there I fell into conversation with a clerk who had served as signalman with General Rohr at Belleau Wood, and he gladly furnished me with the present version. Instead of Able, Baker, Charlie, Dog, and so forth, the phonetic alphabet in use in the army to-day is now Alpha, Bravo, Charlie, Delta, Echo, and so forth."

Lestride shook his head. "I still fail to understand what that might possibly have to do with the message there on the table!"

"Let us consider that message, in view of what I have just revealed to you, Inspector," Homes said evenly. " 'BARCLAYS WEDNESDAY MIDNIGHT SOUP YOUR RESPONSIBILITY QUICKLOCK-TYPE VAULT.' The words in themselves have no meaning, but were used merely to transmit the message by the use of the initial letter of each word. Let us take them, and we see we have B, W, M, S, Y, R, Q, T, and V."

"So?" Lestride demanded, his old belligerence beginning to return.

"So let us see where these letters lead us when we apply them to the modern phonetic alphabet in use to-day, a copy of which I have here." Homes laid a second sheet beside the first one and pointed out the code words for each of the letters. With wonder we saw the message, which Homes wrote for us in his fine copperplate:

BRAVO! "WHISKY" MIKE SIERRA, YANKEE ROMEO, QUEBEC TANGO VICTOR!

"Homes!" I cried proudly. "You have done it again!"

"You mean—" Lestride faltered.

"Precisely," Homes said a bit severely. "Mr. Black was simply carrying this message, received, I have small doubt, from their Canadian correspondent. I do not claim the news is of world-shaking importance, but one thing is certain: delayed as it has been through the heavy-handed tactics of the police, it is undoubtedly no longer newsworthy, and Mr. Black has probably lost money because of it. You might consider this fact when you release him."

"I shall apologize to him most thoroughly as soon as I return to the Yard," Lestride said brokenly, and left our presence a more sober and, I hope, a more judicious man.

It was early morning and a strong wind during the night had cleared the heavy clouds, bringing us welcome relief from the poor weather that had plagued us. I was at the breakfast table shelling my first caper and attempting to peruse the morning journal at the same time, when Homes joined me. He looked pleased with himself, as well he might, having just saved a poor innocent from further incarceration. He seated himself across from me and drew his napkin into his lap.

"And have you found anything in the news of interest to a rather bored investigator, Watney?" he asked, reaching for the kippers and the marmalade.

"Well, Homes, there is this," I said, reading a front-page story. "It seems that last night one of the largest banks in London was burgled. The thieves managed to explode the safe and escape with several million pounds. Police have found some substance on the property which their chemists claim to be a combination of nitrate and glycerol."

"Nitrate, of course," Homes said thoughtfully, "is the reduced charge for telegrams after a certain hour, but glycerol?"

He eschewed his kipper for a few moments to go

into his study and return with a reference volume from his vast library. He leafed through the pages, muttering to himself, and then suddenly stopped as he located the material he sought.

"Ah, here it is! Glycerol: ' . . . used as a softener in pharmacy, as a preservative of food, as a moistener of tobacco and other materials, as an adulterant for wine, beer, etcetera'—"

His eyes came up to meet mine, horrified.

"As an *adulterant* for wine or beer? These miscreants must be brought to the bar of justice posthaste, Watney! A telegram to the authorities offering my services, if you will!"